MW01105049

A MAN FOR MARCY

Books By Rosamond du Jardin

Tobey Heydon Books

Practically Seventeen (1949)
Class Ring (1951)
Boy Trouble (1953)
The Real Thing (1956)
Wedding in the Family (1958)
One of the Crowd (1961)

Marcy Rhodes Books:

Wait for Marcy (1950)
Marcy Catches Up (1952)
A Man for Marcy (1954)
Senior Prom (1957)

Pam & Penny Howard Books:

Double Date (1951)
Double Feature (1953)
Showboat Summer (1955)
Double Wedding (1959)

Non-Series Titles

Someone to Count on (1962)
Young and Fair (1963)
Junior Year Abroad (1960)

Adult Novels

All is Not Gold (1935)
Only Love Lasts (1937)
Honorable Estate (1943)
Brief Glory (1944)
Tomorrow Will Be Fair (1946)

ROSAMOND Du JARDIN

A Man for Marcy

Image Cascade Publishing

www.ImageCascade.com

First *Image Cascade Publishing* edition published 2003.

Library of Congress Cataloging in Publication Data
Du Jardin, Rosamond 1902-1963.
    A man for marcy.

(Juvenile Girls)
Reprint. Originally published: New York & Philadelphia: J. B.
Lippincott Company, 1954.

ISBN 978-1-930009-76-9

To Isabelle and Bill with love.

NOTE:

The origin of the lines of verse on page
91 is the poem "High Flight," by John
Gillespie Magee Jr., a young American
flyer killed in action with the royal
Canadian air force.

CONTENTS

CONTENTS

A MAN FOR MARCY

❧ ONE ❧

Last Date

FRESH FROM HER SHOWER, HER NEWLY donned white slip making her summer-tanned skin look even darker by contrast, Marcy Rhodes stood in the open doorway of her closet frowning thoughtfully at the dresses hanging therein. Early September was such an in-between sort of season, it made choosing a dress for a very special occasion rather difficult. Her leftover summer clothes looked too limp and pastel and her new fall things far too wintery and heavy.

So far as the weather was concerned, it was still summer. The breeze gently billowing the ruffled curtains at Marcy's bedroom windows was as mild as July. It might have been a midsummer wind except that it was laced faintly with the smell of leaf smoke rather than roses. Marcy sniffed, her faint frown deepening. There was some flower fragrance. She smiled realizing that what she smelled was the cologne she had splashed on rather lavishly after her bath. Not too lavishly, she hoped, sniffing a trifle dubiously. But Steve loved Lily of the Valley—he was always saying so. And the fragrance of cologne wasn't too lasting.

Marcy padded over to the window, the white shag rug tickling the soles of her bare feet, and peered out at the night as though expecting it to supply her with an answer to her clothes problem. There was a big fat moon floating like a beach ball above a lake of clouds. Thank goodness for that, anyway. It would have been too foul if, instead of moonlight, there had been rain on the night of her last date with Steve Judson before his departure for college. She couldn't see any stars from her window, but maybe there'd be some later. There should be stars, too, Marcy felt.

"You'd think I was planning a stage setting," she admonished herself, just under her breath. And had to smile again at her own silliness.

She marched firmly back to the closet and without further dillydallying chose a charcoal-gray cotton dress with a crisp white pique collar. She zipped herself into it with brisk, no-nonsense-now movements. She slid her feet into black, high-heeled pumps and sat on the edge of the skirted stool at her dressing table to brush her shining soft dark hair into a cap of casual curls. She selected a scarlet lipstick from the row of varied containers on the dressing table's glass top and applied it carefully, then leaned back to judge the effect.

A voice from behind her made her jump. "You'll do," it said drily. "Don't go getting carried away."

Marcy swung around to face her brother Ken, standing tall in the doorway draped in a big white bathtowel.

His light brown hair was in wet points from his shower, his grin teasing.

"You!" Marcy scolded, but not very severely. "It's about as private around here as Grand Central Station!"

"Can I help it," Ken asked, "if the way from the bathroom leads past your door and you never remember to shut it? Anyhoo, I figured you should be decent by this time. Steve'll be along soon and you couldn't keep the poor guy waiting tonight."

"Oh, I could," Marcy said lightly. "But maybe I won't."

"Better be careful," Ken warned wickedly. "Just think, after tomorrow Steve and I will have a whole new crop of beautiful babes to pick from." He flexed his muscles and emitted a low wolf growl. "You local females better treat us right tonight, or we'll forget you as soon as we hit that campus."

"Is that a threat or a promise?" Marcy inquired.

"You mean you're not worried?" Ken demanded in mock horror. "Rosemary is. She's been so sweet to me our last few dates, I'm practically sure she's shaking in her slippers. I had a hunch Steve was getting the same treatment from you."

Marcy grinned, getting to her feet. "Well, maybe I haven't been quite as rough on him as usual." She asked then, "Is it going to do us any good, Rosemary and me, do you suppose?"

"Depends on what you mean by good," Ken told her. "Rosemary and I know darned well our relationship isn't for keeps. No strings, no regrets, thanks for the memory and all that sort of stuff, that's us. We're the realistic, sensible type. As for you and Steve—well, that's your business."

"Gee, thanks," Marcy said. "That's real big of you to let us handle it."

"I figured you could," Ken admitted amicably. He hitched his towel toga more firmly about his middle, and his blue eyes, looking into Marcy's upturned dark ones, were penetrating. "You've got more sense than you used to have a while back."

"A left-handed compliment if I ever heard one." Marcy made a little face at him. "Scram now, will you, so I can finish getting ready?"

"You're ready enough," Ken told her, ambling off down the hall toward his own room. "What are you trying to do, keep poor old Steve from going to college tomorrow?"

He didn't expect an answer and Marcy didn't make one. She could hear Ken banging around, getting dressed for his date with Rosemary. The small hum of his new electric razor. The thud as he dropped a shoe. The tuneless whistling that meant his spirits were high.

She and Ken understood each other so well, Marcy thought as she took one last reassuring look at herself in the full-length mirror on her closet door. Having a brother only a little over a year older than you was an experience she was glad she hadn't missed. Oh, she'd been mad at Ken often enough. They had scrapped and argued, as brothers and sisters will. Ken had teased, had given her unwanted advice, and she'd resented it. But always between them there'd been a depth of understanding, a warmth of affection, a closeness. They'd stood together against all comers when they were little.

And now that they were almost grown up they still knew they could depend on each other.

There should be violins playing soft music, Marcy thought wryly. I'm getting positively mellow. Lots of times I could have wrung his neck and no doubt he's often felt the same. It's just that the big lug's leaving for college tomorrow and I know darned well I'm going to miss him!

There was no point in trying to deny that, especially to herself. She'd miss Ken and it would seem strange and sort of empty around home without him. After all, he'd been there during all of Marcy's seventeen years. Naturally his departure would leave quite a hole in the fabric of her life. And Steve Judson was going to leave another hole.

With the thought, Marcy heard the chime of the doorbell and, after a moment, her mother's warm friendly voice asking Steve in. Mom liked Steve, Marcy knew. So did Dad. Long before Marcy and Steve had gotten vitally interested in each other, Steve had been Ken's good friend. So in a way he almost seemed like one of the family to her parents. And if she didn't get downstairs pretty quickly, he'd be all involved in conversation with them and it wouldn't be an easy matter to break away. Ordinarily Marcy wouldn't have minded, but tonight had a big SPECIAL sign hung on it. Tonight she didn't even feel like sharing Steve with her parents for a little while. She wanted him all to herself and as quickly as possible.

Mom was still talking with Steve in the hall and Dad, pipe in hand, had come as far as the living-room doorway to join in the conversation when Marcy reached the head of the stairs. Lila and George Rhodes were pleasant-looking, middle-aged people; Lila a bit plump, her fair hair only slightly gray; George thin and black-haired, with warm dark eyes rather like Marcy's looking through shell-rimmed bifocals. Steve towered above Lila. He was six feet tall, slim, with nice broad shoulders and dark hair and eyes. Marcy felt a breathlessness, a sense of excitement, just looking down at the top of his head. The three of them down there were discussing Steve's and Ken's imminent departure and the fact that it would be nice for them both, going to the same college.

"Neither of you should be lonesome," Mom was saying with her quick animated smile.

Dad chuckled and said, "They won't have time for that."

Marcy came skimming down the stairs then, scarcely feeling them under her feet even in high heels, and Steve looked around and grinned at her. "Hi, Marce."

"Hi." She smiled up at him and found it not too easy to pull her eyes away.

Dad said, "They'll keep you so busy, between studies and rushing and getting settled and all—" his tone took on a reminiscent flavor. "I'll never forget my first days at college! There I was, from a little town in California where I knew every living soul, set down on the campus of one of the biggest universities in the country. I tell you, things happened so fast it made my head spin."

If Dad got really started on his college days, Marcy thought with something akin to desperation, they'd be held up forever! It wasn't that she didn't love him, or wasn't, normally, interested in what had happened to him, even if it had been perfect ages ago. But tonight—

Before she could even send a pleading look at her mother, Lila Rhodes said with a little rippling laugh, "Now, George, don't go spoiling the suspense for him. Let him find out for himself."

Marcy's look turned to one of gratitude as her mother's bright blue glance met hers. Mom was such a swell person. She always grasped a situation so quickly, even situations like the present one, which had scarcely had a chance to develop yet. Dad was wonderful, too, of course. It was just that he didn't stop to think sometimes. But Marcy didn't know of a single set of parents, among those possessed by any of her friends, that she had ever felt a remote desire to swap hers for.

Dad said, "Yes—well—maybe you're right, Lila." He flashed Marcy a ruefully apologetic look. "Where are you kids off to?"

"Oh," Steve answered, "I got the car tonight. My folks said I could use it before I even asked. I suppose they figured it'd be the last time for a while." He grinned. "Guess we'll drive around some, go some place for a bite to eat, maybe catch the show at the drive-in. We won't be too late."

Dad nodded, but didn't say anything, tamping down the tobacco in his pipe in a thoughtful, almost absent-minded manner. Maybe, Marcy thought, he was remembering how it had been the night before he left home for college. Had he had a girl then, she wondered. It hadn't been Mom. Dad had been through college when he met Mom. The realization made a queer little cold feeling settle around Marcy's heart. Would Steve look back sometime and remember her just as a girl he had liked pretty well, or had thought he liked, when he was quite young?

Mom said, "It's nice of your parents to drive Ken down, too, when they take you to school. Your mother was telling me today they're planning to leave early tomorrow morning."

"Yeah," Steve said. "It'll take about four hours, and Dad wants to get back home before dark. He hates night driving." He asked then, looking at Marcy, "You all ready?"

She nodded. She had been ready from the second she came downstairs.

"Hadn't you better take a jacket?" Mom asked. "It gets pretty cool these nights."

"It's warm," Marcy demurred. "We'll be in the car."

But Steve, with the ease of long acquaintance, opened the hall closet door and took out her yellow fleece shorty. He gave her shoulders a little tight squeeze as he draped it across them. "Mind your mother."

Dad told them good night and Mom added her customary parting remark, "Have fun."

Going down the walk toward the Judsons' car, her fingers close in Steve's, Marcy thought that the familiar words didn't, somehow, quite fit the occasion.

❧ TWO ❧

Sentimental Journey

"WELL," STEVE SAID, HIS VOICE A BIT HUSKY, "this is it."

He had helped Marcy into the car much more carefully than usual, as though she were very fragile, then had gone around to slide in under the wheel and slam the door. You always had to slam the left front door of the Judsons' car, or it wouldn't catch. Marcy knew that from having ridden in it so often with Steve. But after tonight—

Her throat choked up at the thought and she murmured, her voice little and forlorn, "Our last date."

"Don't say that!" Steve growled at her. "It sounds as if we're never going to see each other again."

"We aren't for a long while." Marcy began counting the months off on her fingers, "September, October, November—"

Steve grabbed her hand and held it to make her stop. "No use getting morbid about it. We're together now, aren't we? Let's not spoil tonight."

"I'm sorry," Marcy said. But she felt morbid.

"I started it," Steve admitted, managing a grin. "The way we should do is just forget about tomorrow. Pretend this is nothing but a regular date, like any other."

Marcy nodded. She could try, but it wouldn't be easy. "Okay," she said, "it's just a date."

"Where'll we go?" Steve asked. "You name it."

"No, you," Marcy said. "I don't care, really."

"Big help you are," Steve told her.

He turned the ignition switch, pressed the starter and backed the car out of the driveway and onto the road. "Any movies around you want to see?"

"I didn't check on what was playing."

"Neither did I," Steve said. "I don't want to see a show much—unless you do?"

Marcy shook her head. Steve steered the car around a corner and Marcy felt herself slide a little closer to him. Their shoulders were touching now and the contact made her feel warmer, less forlorn.

"I don't care a hoot what we do," Steve told her, "so long as we're together. Shall we just drive around awhile?"

"Let's," Marcy said. And then she added, struck by a sudden idea, "Drive over past the Park House."

"You mean you want to play table tennis?" Steve sounded surprised.

"Of course not," Marcy denied. "I didn't mean we'd go in. Just drive past."

Steve shrugged, not getting it. One of those who-knows-what-goes-on-in-the-minds-of-women shrugs.

"I have an idea of something we could do," Marcy

explained. "Only, if I tell you, you'll probably think I'm silly."

Steve grinned at her. "Take a chance and tell me."

"It would be sort of sentimental, I guess." Marcy felt her face getting warm with embarrassment.

"I like my women sentimental," Steve told her and gave her hand a little squeeze. "Go on, tell me. What'll we do?"

"Let's just drive around," Marcy suggested slowly, "past all the places we've got especially nice memories about, places where we've had a lot of fun. Like the Park House."

She wondered if Steve remembered that the very first time he'd paid any attention to her had been over a hot game of table tennis at the Park House. He had stopped by at the Rhodeses one Saturday afternoon to get Ken to play a game with him. Or, at least, that had been his excuse. But Ken hadn't been at home. Marcy had, though, and the upshot had been that she and Steve played table tennis that afternoon. And somehow that occasion had marked the end of Steve's seeming to consider her merely as Ken's kid sister, too young to waste time on. More than a year ago, that had been, Marcy realized. Almost a year and a half. If Steve didn't remember the Park House's special significance, she couldn't really blame him. But she hoped he did.

"Yeah," Steve said thoughtfully, "that would be a good idea. Sort of a sentimental journey, as the song says."

Marcy nodded.

"Starting at the Park House," Steve went on, still in

that slow, reminiscent tone, "because that's where we started really. Funny to think back, isn't it?"

"I wasn't sure you'd remember," Marcy told him.

"Gee, yes," Steve said positively. "It was queer that day, how different you seemed to me than you ever had before."

"You, too," Marcy told him. "Up until then you were just a friend of Ken's, nobody to give a second thought to."

It all seemed so long ago now, so infinitely far away. So many things had happened since, so many dates, dances and parties and movies and just riding around, as they were doing now. And their big break-up this summer over Noel Cramer, the boy in Colorado Marcy had met on her vacation. If they could get together again after a quarrel like that, the feeling between them must be real and lasting. If only, Marcy thought desolately, Steve weren't going away tomorrow—

His thoughts must have followed the same pattern hers had. Because Steve said aloud, his voice husky again, "Gee, Marce, I'm going to miss you."

"Me, too," Marcy admitted. "But let's not think about it now. What good will it do?"

"None, I guess," Steve admitted. "Where'll we drive next on this safari of ours?"

"You pick the next place," Marcy told him.

"School," Steve decided. "Not because I love the crumby old place so much. But that's where the G. A. A. dance was held—the one you finally screwed up your courage to invite me to."

They both laughed, remembering. And Marcy added, "I wore my white formal, the one Grandmother sent me for Christmas that year after I hinted so in my letter to her."

"It sort of sparkled," Steve recalled. "You made quite an impression on me that night."

"Oh, I don't know about that," Marcy teased. She wondered how she was able to keep her tone so light when she was unhappily aware of all the attractive girls in stunning formals Steve would soon be exposed to at college.

"I'm still hanging around," Steve reminded her.

But not for long, Marcy thought desolately. She didn't say the words aloud, though. She tried not to think them. Instead, she suggested brightly that they drive past the outdoor movie, since they'd spent a lot of pleasant evenings there.

"Okay," Steve agreed, "as soon as we take a last look at the old school."

"Last look?" Marcy repeated wryly. "I've got another year there—remember?"

The realization gave her a strange, almost panicky feeling. Another year at High without Steve, or Ken—it certainly would be different. She'd scarcely had time yet to become fully aware of the change. High school had only started last Wednesday and so far her school hours had been so full of registering and buying books, of getting accustomed to new courses and different teachers, that she hadn't had much time for thinking about anything other than the mere mechanics of starting a new semester. And, of course, Steve and her brother weren't actually gone yet. They were still around to see and have fun with when school time was over. Next week would be harder, Marcy reminded herself. Much harder.

"It's funny," Steve said, stopping the car in front of the sprawling brick façade of Westfield High, "what a different perspective you get on your high-school years when they're over."

"I suppose so," Marcy agreed.

The familiar old building looked strange by moonlight. Black shadows deepened its angles. Its windows were dark, like hundreds of closed eyes, sleeping. Even the curving walk along which Marcy had hurried to the front entrance so many, many times, had a mysterious look, half-hidden by its sheltering row of bushes. Marcy's glance lifted to the sky above the building. As she had hoped earlier, a lot of stars had come out. They reminded her of some lines of verse, something they had memorized in Freshman English for a poetry project and which Marcy had not forgotten.

> The night has a thousand eyes,
> And the day but one;
> Yet the light of the bright world dies
> With the dying sun.

She didn't say the lines aloud, though. Steve had too good a memory. He just might recall the rest of the poem, which went:

> The mind has a thousand eyes,
> And the heart but one;
> Yet the light of a whole life dies,
> When love is done.

Marcy felt herself flushing a little at the mere thought of Steve imagining she was *that* sentimental.

After a few minutes they drove on. They went past

the drive-in, as Marcy had suggested, and past Liz Kendall's house, since Liz was Marcy's closest friend and the whole crowd had had so many good parties in the Kendall's rumpus room. It was Steve's idea to drive all the way out to the lake, where he and Marcy had met again after their quarrel last month, and had made up. He parked the car on a little bluff overlooking the dark, murmurous water.

"Right down there it was," Steve pointed toward the sandy beach. "That's where we made up."

Marcy nodded and Steve's arm went around her and she rested her head against his shoulder. "I'm glad we did."

"So am I," Steve said, "only—it would have been even better if we hadn't scrapped at all. Think of the time we wasted, being mad."

"Silly of us, wasn't it?" Marcy agreed.

But Steve had been jealous of her interest in Noel, even though the other boy was hundreds of miles away in Colorado. And Marcy's own attitude, a bit dazzled as she still had been with her vacation romance, hadn't helped any.

Steve said seriously, "There's one thing I think we ought to get straight, Marce, before I go away tomorrow. I realize now I was pretty stupid to get sore about you and the Cramer guy, when you were 'way out west and I was here. I couldn't expect you to just sit around, not having any dates, or fun, because we weren't together. And I want you to know I'm not going to be like that when I go to college. You can date other guys and I won't say a word. Honest."

Perversely, Marcy felt a little surge of disappointment.

She knew it was unreasonable, but she couldn't seem to help it. Annoyed as she had been over Steve's jealousy, it had been flattering. Still, his attitude now was much more sensible. How had Ken put it only a little while ago, in describing his and Rosemary Ames's relationship? "No strings, no regrets, thanks for the memory and all that sort of stuff, that's us." Was it Steve and she, too, Marcy wondered? And something like a chill wind blew across her heart, making her shiver.

"You cold?" Steve asked solicitously.

But Marcy shook her head. She said, "That's the real·istic way to look at things, I guess. I'll date other boys and you'll date other girls and—just forget each other."

"Now wait a minute," Steve objected. "I didn't mean anything like that. We're going to write, aren't we?"

"I thought we were, but—"

"It's all settled," Steve said firmly. "But about dating —well, it's going to be pretty grim for you all senior year if you don't date other fellows. And, to be frank, I won't have much fun at college if I don't go out with any girls. But—I could never forget you, Marcy. You ought to know that. And I'm figuring on asking you down to the big dances at school and all—if you'll come—"

Marcy felt Steve's arm tighten around her and her heart quickened as she lifted her lips for his kiss. Why did she always have to be so contrary about everything? He was only trying to work things out in the best and happiest way for both of them.

She told him, "Of course, I'll come, if you ask me. I don't know why I said that about forgetting each other. I didn't really mean it."

"I couldn't forget you if I tried," Steve told her, his

voice low and not quite steady. "You're the one, Marce. You always will be. But so long as we're going to be apart, I was only trying to figure it the best way for both of us."

"Of course," Marcy said. "I know that."

They sat for a while, talking, hearing the croak of frogs and the gentle lapping of the water on the beach below. Then they drove back to town for a final soda at the Sweet Shop, where they had had so many sodas before. Several of their crowd were already assembled in the big corner booth, Rosemary and Ken, Liz and Bill Weaver, a couple of others.

"Join us," Ken invited, with a large airy gesture. "Drown your sorrows in a double chocolate malted or something. Eat, drink and be merry—"

"For tomorrow we get left flat," Rosemary finished wryly. "We'll be just the girls you left behind you."

"I'll bet," Bill said, his quizzical glance on Liz, who was the fickle type. "You'll probably have a whole new crop of men buzzing around before we're out of sight."

Everyone laughed and there was much kidding and even more noise than usual. But Marcy sensed something hollow about all the gayety, a little undercurrent of genuine sadness. Feeling Steve's fingers close around hers under the sheltering edge of the table, Marcy was glad they'd had that talk on the bluff above the lake in the starlit darkness. That was their real good-bye.

THREE

Being a Senior Is Dull

MARCY WAITED FOR LIZ IN THE CORRIDOR at school, just inside the front entrance. She had her math book under one arm, her raincoat across the other, ready to slip into as soon as her friend appeared. It was a drab, sodden sort of day and the tile floor of the entry was tracked with dried mud from the passage of many feet. Even though it was Friday afternoon and Marcy was quite aware there'd be no school for two days, her spirits remained almost as heavy as the weather. So it was Friday. So what? Marcy thought disinterestedly. Week ends just weren't as much fun as they used to be.

Steve had been gone two weeks now. Or it would be two weeks Sunday. It seemed much longer—months and months, Marcy thought wistfully. She had had two letters from him, if you could call them letters. The first had been scarcely a page long, just a brief note telling her how busy he was with placement tests, getting settled, and fraternity rushing. He promised to write more

next time. But the letter Marcy had got from him yesterday hadn't been much better. Oh, it was a bit longer
and there was a little more news in it. He and Ken,
Steve had written, had been lucky enough to get tapped
for the same fraternity. College courses were murder,
he'd informed her, implying that high school was a complete snap by comparison. He'd been able to arrange his
class schedule so that he could sleep till eight-thirty, but
Ken had to get up an hour earlier. Some of the professors
were okay, but some were Characters, with a capital C.
There had been a couple of lines about the foul weather
they were having, a sketchy description of some of the
main points of interest on campus. And he'd finished up
with, "I miss you like anything. Love, Steve." That last
line, Marcy reflected bleakly, had been the only really
personal thing about the whole letter. And even so,
reading words like that wasn't at all the same as hearing
Steve say them.

The letter had left her with an empty, unsatisfied feeling. There had been no reminiscing in it about Westfield, or any of the things she and Steve had done
together while he was still at home. It was as though he
had moved into a world entirely apart from all the familiar scenes they had known together, as though he
had left the past behind him.

And I'm a part of the past, Marcy thought unhappily.
She wondered if he'd only added that last line, the one
she cherished so, because he'd felt sorry for her, left out
of the bright new life he obviously found so engrossing.

It was a relief to see Liz approaching. They could
have a good gab-session on the way home. She and Liz
had been friends so long they never held anything back

from each other. And Liz was even worse off than she. Bill Weaver had gone all the way to Texas to college. And Liz hadn't had a letter from him yet. They could, in effect, cry on each other's shoulders, Marcy thought, and the prospect made her feel a little better.

Liz didn't look in the least downhearted as she came breezing up. The blond hair framing her alert pretty face was naturally curly, so the rain had tightened it becomingly. Her bright red jacket imparted an illusion of gayety, too.

"Guess who offered us a lift home," she exclaimed, as Marcy shrugged into her raincoat. "Bix Meyers. I just ran into him and he said he'd duck out to the parking lot, get his heap and meet us around in front in five minutes."

Marcy saw little cause for such enthusiasm. "You sound as if riding in that wreck of Bix's is a big deal. I'll bet the top leaks—that is, if he can get the top up."

"Better than walking in the rain," Liz pointed out philosophically. "Come on. He'll probably be there by the time we are."

Marcy doubted it. Still she had little choice but to pull the hooded collar of her coat up over her head and follow Liz out and down the walk to the street. As she had more than half expected, Bix was nowhere in sight.

"So what do we do?" Marcy asked in annoyance. "Stand here waiting?"

"You are in a mood!" Liz said. "Here he comes now."

Bix's old convertible chugged noisily around the corner and came to a splashing stop a few feet from them. The faded top was up and Bix exclaimed cheerfully as he leaned over to open the door, "Hop in, you lucky creatures! Don't know why I'm being so good to you."

Marcy was too annoyed about her cold wet ankles to kid back. But Liz laughed, "It's your noble nature, or our winning charm. I'm not sure which."

Bix was a big, easygoing sort of boy, with brassy blond hair and sometimes an almost overwhelming sense of humor. He was given to violent sport shirts, harmless practical jokes and a conviction, real or pretended, that all girls found him utterly irresistible. Marcy didn't mind him ordinarily, she'd even had a few dates with him long ago, but now she was in no mood for his type of clowning.

Liz, apparently, was. She and Bix kept up a running crossfire of outrageous kidding and laughter, to which Marcy listened glumly and without the least appreciation. How could Liz enjoy such silly, corny humor, she wondered?

"How about stopping at the Sweet Shop?" Bix suggested. "I'll treat if you'll settle for a Coke."

Marcy declined, saying she had to get home early. She fully expected Liz to do likewise.

But Liz coaxed, "Oh, come on, Marce. What have you got to do that's so important it can't wait half an hour?"

"I promised to help Mom with some stuff," Marcy fibbed, her annoyance with the weather and Bix expanding to include Liz as well. "Thanks, anyway. You can just drop me off."

And that was exactly what Bix and Liz proceeded to do. There went her talk with Liz, Marcy thought, as the car door slammed behind her and the old convertible sloshed off down the street in the direction of the Sweet

Shop. How could Liz waste her time on Bix when she didn't care a snap about him, Marcy wondered? She herself felt fed to the teeth with him and she couldn't understand why Liz cared to linger in his company.

Marcy moved slowly up the walk to her front door, skirting the puddles absently. Wouldn't it be wonderful if there was another letter from Steve waiting for her on the hall table, where Mom always left her mail? The thought lifted Marcy's spirits a little, improbable as it seemed. She'd had a letter from Steve yesterday, one she hadn't even answered yet. Still, mightn't he have realized what an unsatisfactory sort of letter it had been, full of college activities and practically nothing else? It was possible he'd felt an urge to write her again the very next day, to tell her he was having trouble getting her out of his mind, that her face kept coming between him and his books when he tried to study. Maybe he'd written that he was homesick, that he didn't see how he was going to stick it out till Thanksgiving without seeing her.

Marcy hurried across the porch and opened the front door expectantly. But there was no letter at all on the hall table. She caught a glimpse of her disappointed face in the mirror above it and turned away quickly, feeling anger at her own silliness rise in her.

You knew there wouldn't be one, she admonished herself. You're just crazy, building up to a letdown like that!

She put down her book and slipped out of her raincoat, hung it in the hall closet. The house had an empty feel. "Mom?" Marcy called tentatively.

There was no answer. Her hunch had been correct. Oh, fine, Marcy thought. Just dandy!

Almost, but not quite, she wished she had let Liz and Bix persuade her to stop at the Sweet Shop. Still, even with Mom away somewhere, she was glad she'd come home. If only Liz had come, too, so they could have talked. Marcy felt an overwhelming need to talk to someone. Maybe the need could be satisfied by writing a letter to Steve.

But when she had gone upstairs to her own pleasant room, had got out her stationery and pen and sat down on the chaise longue with it, all urge to write deserted her. She sat there, staring at the empty sheet of paper, nibbling absently at the smooth top of the pen. What did she have to tell Steve? What was there to say? Nothing of the slightest interest or importance had happened to her since he left. And she was in no frame of mind to be gay and chatty and entertaining over nothing, as she usually could. Suppose she wrote exactly as she felt. Experimentally, Marcy let the pen's tip touch the paper. When she had written a couple of lines, she stopped and stared at them.

"Dear Steve: I feel lower than an angleworm's tummy—"

Now wouldn't Steve be intrigued to hear that, Marcy thought wryly? She ran her pen almost viciously through the words and began drawing silly doodles. The wind blew rain against the windows with a desolate, sighing sound. Why didn't Mom come home, Marcy wondered. Where had she gone? A vague recollection of something her mother had mentioned at breakfast drifted into her mind. Something about a Hospital Guild meeting that afternoon. Of course, that was where Mom was. Before her marriage Lila Rhodes had been a nurse and she had kept up an active interest in nursing and medicine all her life. Neighbors were always summoning her in emergencies of illness or accident. Even aside from her nursing knowledge, she was one of those calm, competent, understanding people it was good to have around.

I'd like her around right now, Marcy thought glumly. I'd like anyone around, for that matter.

She realized with a sharp pang that she was missing her brother Ken almost as much as Steve. All her life she'd had Ken around. Now, with him gone, even home didn't seem the same.

Almost without her pushing it, the pen in Marcy's fingers wrote, "The rain tapped at the windows with chill fingers, crying, sighing—"

Poetry, Marcy thought! I'm really sunk when I begin writing sad poetry to pass the time.

She pushed the paper aside almost desperately, before she began trying to think of another line to rhyme with the first one. How long she had been sitting there, Marcy had no idea. But the room had darkened perceptibly. She got up and went around switching on lights. As she passed it, she turned the knob of her little radio and, a moment later, an announcer's rich, persuasive voice poured like syrup out into the room, extolling the marvelous powers of some new laundry detergent.

"Just what I need," Marcy answered him aloud, turning the dial till she found some music.

Above its soothing rhythms, she heard the front door open and her mother's voice call, "Marcy?"

"I'll be right down," Marcy answered relievedly.

Lila Rhodes was putting her coat away as Marcy swooped down the stairs. Mom ran her fingers through her crisp, graying hair, pushing it into place after the confining influence of her hat.

She said, smiling at Marcy, "The house was all dark as I drove up. I thought no one was home. Then the light went on in your room as I came out of the garage. You just get here?"

Marcy nodded, letting it go at that. Of what use to tell Mom she had been brooding in the dark, feeling morose and sorry for herself?

Mom chattered on, heading for the kitchen, with Marcy close at her heels, "The Guild meeting lasted longer than usual. It was interesting though. Doctor Fairfax spoke. I don't suppose you've had time to start dinner?"

Marcy shook her head. "I'm sorry." She really was sorry she hadn't thought about dinner. It would have been something to do.

Mom said, "I have a casserole all ready. You'd have seen it if you'd looked out in the kitchen. I even left a note for you on the oven, telling you when to turn it on."

"What can I do now?" Marcy asked.

Mom tied a bright plaid apron around her waist, then turned to flash her warm smile at Marcy. "I'm not calling you down, honey. The casserole will have plenty of time to bake before Dad gets home. I know how busy you are at school, your last year and all. I remember how busy Ken was." She gave Marcy a little hug as she passed her, heading for the refrigerator. "Is it as exciting as you expected, being a senior?"

Marcy stared at Mom, at her animated, smiling face. It seemed a shame to disillusion her, when she obviously thought that Marcy must be having a wonderful time. But there were limits to how much she could take, and those limits had been reached.

Marcy said flatly, firmly, "Being a senior is just about the dullest thing that ever happened to me."

❧ FOUR ❦

The Widows

WHEN DAD GOT HOME FROM WORK, MARCY and Mom were still discussing the subject of why Marcy found being a senior dull. It took him only a few minutes to get the gist of the conversation and join in. They kicked it around during most of dinner.

"Are you making an effort, dear?" Mom asked. "Of course, it's only natural for you to miss Steve and Ken, too. But if you join things, clubs and all that, take part in the various activities—well, you'll make new friends to take the place of the ones who are away."

Mom made it sound so simple. She was trying to be helpful, Marcy knew. But parents just couldn't seem to understand about some things. It had been too long since they themselves had been young.

"The trouble is," Marcy tried to explain, "Liz and I have always gone out with boys a year older. That's what makes it so rough on us—on me," she corrected, remembering Liz's silly concentration on Bix this afternoon. "The kids my own age—well, they seem so young and not very interesting after Steve, and Noel this summer. I just can't seem to get very excited about any of them."

"But clubs—" Mom began.

"Oh, I've joined some," Marcy broke in. She was in Journalism Club and Spanish, too. The meetings were interesting enough, but nothing to arouse mad enthusiasm. She added, with a little shrug, "The kids in them seem pretty infantile, too."

"Still," Mom commented, "it's something to occupy your time."

Not enough of it, Marcy thought.

Dad asked, pushing his coffee cup toward Mom for a refill, "These classmates you speak of, who are so infantile—I take it you mean boys?"

Marcy nodded. "The girls are much more mature. Oh, some of the boys act grown up enough, but not very many. And most of those are either going steady, or they're so popular they've got all the girls chasing them and it's gone to their heads."

"Are you sure," Mom asked, "that you're not just generalizing? You can't know every single boy in your class well enough to pass judgment."

Marcy said, "I know them as well as I want to." And then, because that wasn't a very logical statement, or even an entirely true one, she asked, her voice a little plaintive, "Do we have to go on talking and talking about it? I'll get along all right. Don't worry."

Mom smiled at her and Dad's glance was sympathetic. "We just want you to have fun," he said.

And Mom seconded, "Your last year in high school is

a time for fun. We don't want anything to spoil that for you."

They let the subject drop then. Mom got to talking about the Guild meeting. "They're so terribly short-handed at the hospital," she said regretfully. "Sometimes I feel a little guilty, being a registered nurse and not doing much of anything with it."

"Now, Lila," Dad said. "Aren't you busy enough taking care of Marcy and me and the house and all, besides being the mainstay of the neighborhood in time of trouble?"

Mom smiled, but her blue eyes were serious. "Lots of nurses at the hospital are married. And some of their children are younger than Marcy."

"Maybe they need the money," Dad pointed out.

"Maybe," Mom admitted. "But they must feel quite a sense of satisfaction, too."

The phone rang then and Marcy, who had already finished her dessert, jumped up to answer it. She left her parents lingering over their coffee and lifted the receiver expectantly. No doubt it was Liz, calling to suggest they go to the movies or do something else together. But it wasn't Liz's voice that answered Marcy's inquiring "Hello?" It turned out to be Ken's girl friend.

"Oh, hi, Rosemary," Marcy murmured. "What do you know?"

"Not much for sure," Rosemary answered. "I was just wondering whether you're busy tonight, or if you could come over. Nothing but a hen session," she added. "Our old club's sort of petered out lately. So some of us were figuring on maybe starting up a new one."

Marcy felt a faint prod of interest. Still, there was Liz to consider. She told Rosemary, "Gee, I'd like to, but I'm expecting to hear from Liz—"

"I called her just a minute ago," Rosemary broke in. There was a slightly wistful note in her voice as she added, "She has a date for tonight."

"A date?" Marcy repeated in surprise.

"The genuine article," Rosemary said.

"Did she tell you who with?"

"Bix Meyers." A little chuckle followed the name along the wire. "No one to make me turn green with envy, but definitely better than nothing."

Bix! Marcy thought. How could Liz waste her time?

The thought occurred to her that she was being a little unfair to Bix. He wasn't absolutely impossible. In fact, she herself used to find him quite amusing. But she had outgrown him. She had supposed Liz had outgrown him, too.

Rosemary was saying, "So if you were figuring on doing anything with Liz, that's out."

"I guess so," Marcy agreed. "I will come over then. What sort of club did you have in mind?"

"Wait till you hear!" Rosemary exclaimed with her usual effervescent enthusiasm. "All the girls who'll be here are kids whose favorite guys have up and left for college, or the service, or something. That includes you, too, doesn't it?"

"That's for sure," Marcy said feelingly.

"Me, too." Rosemary's tone was wistful. "Do you know that darling brother of yours has written me just one measly letter?"

"That's all we've had from him, too," Marcy admitted. "Ken's a horrible letter writer."

But she remembered his telling her how realistic he and Rosemary were, how they both knew their relationship wasn't for keeps. Ken had been very positive about it, but maybe, Marcy realized, Rosemary felt differently.

Now she was going on, "Well, some of us poor deserted females were crying on each other's shoulders after school this afternoon, and we decided we ought to get together and have a club. We're thinking of calling it 'The Widows.' Sound like a good idea to you?"

"Definitely!" Marcy exclaimed.

It was a terrific idea. She felt herself brightening at the mere thought of hobnobbing with a crowd of friends, all in the same boat, all faced with the same problem. Girls like herself, who'd had such fun the last year or so, dating boys a bit older than themselves, not stopping to realize what a spot they'd be in when their favorite men finished school ahead of them and they were left behind.

"Liz'll want to join, too," Marcy told Rosemary confidently.

"The more the merrier," Rosemary said. A note of doubt crept into her voice. "We'd love to have her, but I didn't tell her anything about it when she said she had a date. I thought maybe she and Bix—"

"Don't be silly!" Marcy hooted. "She's known Bix forever, just as the rest of us have. You don't imagine she'd really get interested in him at this late date?"

"Well, I certainly don't think she'll carry a torch for Bill Weaver forever," Rosemary said flatly. "Liz isn't the type. She never pretended to be."

"I know—but Bix!" Marcy had to laugh at the mere idea of Liz and Bix being a really solid twosome. It was too crazy. She told Rosemary firmly, "Of course, she'll want to join 'The Widows.' Tonight is just one of those things . . . "

✬ FIVE ✬

Liz Has Her Own Ideas

MARCY AWOKE, AS WAS HER ANNOYING habit on Saturday mornings, at the same early hour at which she had to get up on school days. But after a moment's drowsy reflection she realized what day it was and turned over for another delicious hour's sleep.

Her parents were halfway through breakfast when she got downstairs. Dad didn't go to the office on Saturday, which was clearly indicated by his plaid sport shirt and disreputable old slacks. But Mom looked her usual trim morning self in red-and-white checked gingham. They both smiled and greeted Marcy as she came into the sunny kitchen, wearing her Saturday uniform of blue jeans and old white shirt, one of her father's long-discarded ones, much frayed at neck and rolled back cuffs.

"Hi," Marcy answered, yawning. "What's for breakfast?"

"Pancakes," Mom told her. "The batter's there in the bowl on the oven. Help yourself."

Marcy proceeded to put a dab of butter on the griddle and drop spoonfuls of batter onto the sizzling pan, until she had a pancake of generous proportions. Having fried it to a delicate golden brown on both sides, she put it on a plate, spread it generously with butter and strawberry preserves, rolled it up and covered the whole with maple syrup and powdered sugar.

"If I ate that," Mom said wistfully as Marcy carried it over to the table and sat down, "I'd gain five pounds. Butter *and* preserves *and* syrup—ah, to be young and slim."

Dad grinned at her. "You're not fat, nor old, either. Just—"

Mom cut in, "If you say pleasingly plump, I'll crown you with the syrup pitcher."

"Just right, was all I was going to say," Dad chuckled. "Any objection to that?"

"You're prejudiced," Mom told him. "I like you that way, but I should lose five pounds, at least—maybe even ten."

"You'd be too skinny then," Dad shook his head.

"If I took a job at the hospital," Mom said thoughtfully, "I'll bet I'd lose some weight. I saw Peggy Morton at the Guild meeting yesterday and she was telling me Ellen Deane's gone back to nursing. Peggy says she's working five days a week and looks perfectly stunning, thinner than she has in years."

"Let's get this straight." Dad's eyes were teasing behind his shell-rimmed glasses. "Are you threatening to go back to nursing because there's such a shortage, or because it would be a sort of stream-lining beauty treatment—with salary?"

Mom laughed. "You know that's not it, George. If there were plenty of younger nurses, I wouldn't even consider it. We don't actually need the money. And it would mean extra work at home for Marcy and sacrifices for you, too, in lots of ways. But the hospital's so desperately shorthanded."

Dad and Mom went on with their discussion. Marcy drank her orange juice and ate her pancake and pork sausages and finished off with a big glass of milk. She paid little heed to her parents' conversation, nor did she take Mom's arguments very seriously. Mom had talked before about going back to nursing, but Dad had always managed to persuade her not to. He'd do it again, Marcy felt sure. And the hospital would get by someway, even with its inadequate staff, just as it always had.

Her own thoughts were busy with other matters. She wanted first of all to talk to Liz, to tell her what a good hen party she'd missed last night by going off on her silly old date with Bix. As soon as she had finished her meal, Marcy jumped up and cleared the table, all but her parents' coffee cups and the percolator.

"I'll clean my room this morning for sure," she told Mom, "and do anything else you want me to. But first I've got to see Liz. Okay if I run over there for half an hour?"

Mom nodded. "Of course." Her voice sounded a shade absent, as though she hadn't really heard what Marcy said. Or at least, as if she hadn't paid much attention to it.

Marcy slipped on her jacket and hurried out into the bright autumn day. The sky was a clear cloudless blue, reminding her fleetingly of the way the sky over Colorado had looked. And thinking of Colorado she was reminded of Noel Cramer. Would she ever see Noel again, Marcy wondered? Probably not. The realization brought a little nostalgic pang in its wake. They'd had such fun together, going on sunrise picnics in the mountains, square dancing in the Cramers' big barn, eating great juicy barbeques at the rodeo and picnic Liz's Uncle Jace had given in her honor and Marcy's. And there'd been auto trips by moonlight and horseback rides in the sunny clear days high on the plateau where Jace Kendall's ranch was located. For a while Marcy had thought herself actually in love with Noel Cramer. But Noel, despite the fact that he was not yet twenty, had been mature in his ideas. He had asked Marcy to marry him. And although she had had the common sense to decline, it would always be, she thought, one of the most thrilling things that had ever happened to her.

But even before she had scuffed through the leaves the short distance to Liz Kendall's house, Marcy's thoughts were centered on Steve again, and Noel was pushed into the background. Steve was her main concern. Thinking about Noel bordered on unreality, like dreaming of some movie star she might have had a crush on. Moreover, Steve was her passport to "The Widows," and the new club was something she could scarcely wait to tell Liz all about.

Her friend looked as though she were on her way to haunt a house as she opened the door. Her faded jeans and old shirt matched Marcy's, but in addition she had her head tied up in a bath towel and there was a smudge of dirt on her nose. "Come on up to my room," she invited. "I'm cleaning it."

"None too soon, either," Mrs. Kendall commented drily from the kitchen. "It's reached the stage where I can't open the door without things falling out in my face."

"Sounds familiar," Marcy called back as she followed Liz up the stairs. "My mother talks the same way about me."

Liz knocked over the dust mop with a clatter as she waved Marcy into her disordered private domain. "Just sit on the floor," she suggested. "It's the only place there's room. My summer clothes aren't all put away yet. My mother's been having fits."

"Mine, too," Marcy admitted. "I've got a clean-up job waiting at home. But I was dying to tell you about last night."

Liz asked, "Did you go to Rosemary's? She called me."

Marcy nodded, flopping down cross-legged on the floor while Liz began halfheartedly sorting a pile of shorts and summer halters on the bed. "It wasn't just a party, though," Marcy explained. And she went on to supply Liz with all the details about the new club. "There were just six of us last night," she finished animatedly, "but we'd like to get eight, all kids whose favorite men are away. And we're going to meet every Friday night and call ourselves 'The Widows.' Don't you love that name?"

Liz considered for a moment. To Marcy's astonishment, she didn't seem enthusiastic at all. "It sounds kind of morbid to me," she admitted finally.

"Oh, don't be so literal!" Marcy exclaimed. "We weren't morbid, at all! We played records and ate popcorn and gabbed. If we get eight, we could play bridge at some meetings."

"But no men?" Liz asked.

"Why, no," Marcy told her. "We're all girls who—"

"You explained about that before," Liz broke in gently. She lifted a pile of clothes, stared at it a moment, then put it down again in the same spot. Her blue eyes were troubled, looking into Marcy's brown ones. "I think you're making a mistake."

"Starting the club, you mean?" Marcy asked blankly. "But, Liz, our old club always used to be such fun."

"I know," Liz nodded. "But it sort of fell apart as we all grew older and began dating. And it never met on Friday, of all times! Why, Friday's one of the best date nights!" She asked then, her tone serious, "Marcy, don't you intend to go out with any boys till Steve gets back?"

Marcy stared at her. She felt disappointed in Liz, definitely annoyed by her reaction. She said, "Oh, I might, if someone exciting asked me. But if it's a choice between 'The Widows' and a date with someone I don't care anything about, I'll take 'The Widows' any time! Just going out with a boy because he's a boy—"

"I suppose," Liz interrupted, a wry smile curving her mouth, "you mean Bix."

"Well, frankly," Marcy admitted, "I was a little surprised at your going out with him last night. A Coke's one thing, and a whole evening's another."

"It sure is," Liz said cheerfully. "We had a swell time. Saw a good movie, had hamburgers afterward at the Lighthouse, where we ran into several other kids we knew. Since when," she demanded, "are you so snooty about a date with Bix? You've gone out with him yourself."

"I know," Marcy said, "but that was before Steve and I—" She broke off to demand, "Surely you can't compare Bix with Bill Weaver?"

"There's one thing I prefer about Bix to Bill," Liz informed her. "He's here, while Bill is far, far away. Anyway, the mere fact that I go out with Bix doesn't mean we're vitally interested in each other. Doesn't it ever cross that one-track mind of yours that it might be a good idea to let the boys around school see that you're back in circulation again? Maybe someone I could like a lot more than Bix might see me with him and realize that I'm not hopelessly nursing a mad pash for Bill. And if you're smart," Liz told her, "you'll follow my shining example, instead of sitting around being blue with a bunch of frustrated females. What a waste of Friday nights!"

"Oh, I wouldn't say that!" Marcy felt her annoyance sharpening. Usually she and Liz saw pretty much eye to eye on any matter. But now Liz seemed determined to be difficult. "The boys at school, this year's crop of seniors—" Marcy expressed her low opinion of them with an eloquent shrug.

Liz asked perversely, "What's wrong with Gary Stiles and Jim Marquardt and Bruce Douglas and—"

"That's not fair," Marcy objected. "You're picking out all the big shots. I mean the majority, not just letter men and those who are so popular they've got half the girls at school chasing them."

But Liz argued, "The majority's okay, too. You're simply spoiled from going around with older fellows. I prefer older ones, too," she admitted frankly. "But can see we made a big mistake to concentrate on them so exclusively. We could be left out on a limb this year if we don't watch out."

Marcy sighed a sigh of sheer exasperation and got to her feet. When Liz was in one of her contrary moods, there was no use arguing with her. "I might as well go home and clean my room, if you're going to be like this," Marcy snapped. "I thought for sure you'd be as interested in starting a new club as the rest of us."

"Not that kind of a club," Liz said flatly. "I think you're all loopy. Why, if you kids don't begin going out with other fellows, you may not even get asked to the Senior Prom!"

"And what's so wonderful about going to the Prom," Marcy demanded, "with some—some infant?"

"Infant or not," Liz said, "they're as old as we are. I'll settle for one of them. At least, I'll be out having fun while you 'widows' sit around rehashing last year's loves and feeling sorry for yourselves!"

Marcy marched down the stairs and out into the crisp sunshine, too angry even to say good-bye. She hadn't felt so disappointed in Liz since they were in the sixth grade and had had a terrific row over whether they should only invite girls to their joint Halloween party. Come to think of it, Marcy realized, that quarrel had been about boys, too. She couldn't help grinning a little at the recollection.

Of course, she wouldn't stay mad at Liz. They were too good friends for that. But why, Marcy wondered, must she be so unreasonable? "The Widows" wasn't going to be nearly so much fun without Liz.

❧ SIX ❧

Mom Makes Up Her Mind

AS MARCY HAD KNOWN WOULD HAPPEN, she and Liz made up their quarrel before the week was out. But neither of them changed her mind, or went over to the other's viewpoint.

There was a night football game at school that Friday, so "The Widows" decided to attend it together in lieu of their regular meeting. Grouped with the others on the wooden bleachers, cheering the Westfield team on to victory, Marcy did a surprised double-take at sight of Liz, seated several rows ahead with a lanky senior named Hank Novak. She knew Liz hadn't had a date for the game up until this morning. Liz herself had admitted as much as she and Marcy walked to school. "I'm still hoping, though," Liz had said.

And her hopes must have come true. But Hank

41

Novak certainly wasn't anyone to get excited about, Marcy felt as she eyed him critically.

Afterwards, Marcy and her friends stopped at the Sweet Shop for malteds. The place was jammed and noisy as usual after a game. A sudden loneliness for Steve caught at Marcy. How many times had they sat over there in one of the booths, sipping sodas, talking, their hands clasped under the shielding edge of the table? So many, Marcy thought, that she half expected to see Steve now, or his ghost. Her mouth twisted into an unsteady smile at the thought. What an idea! The Sweet Shop haunted—why, there wouldn't be room for a self-respecting ghost to squeeze through this mob. And Steve was far away and so busy he never had time to write more than one letter a week. Marcy tried to dismiss him from her mind firmly. But it wasn't easy, in this place of all places.

She began chatting vivaciously with Rosemary and the others as they eased their way through the throng to the soda fountain and gave their orders. Finding a seat was out of the question, so they drank their malteds standing up.

"Hi, all you gorgeous females," Bix Meyers' exuberant voice broke in on them. "What is this, the sextet from luscious, or something?"

Everyone laughed, even Marcy. Bix was funny sometimes.

He edged away from the counter now, though. "Pardon me, but so many women all together are too much for my blood pressure. I have such a low boiling point. I'll take on any one of you singly, but not en masse."

He drifted over to the corner booth and squeezed in with two couples who were eating banana splits. Trust Bix not to be self-conscious about intruding.

"I guess we are a little frightening all in a bunch like this." There was a trace of wistfulness in Rosemary's tone. "Gee, I wish Ken was around! Things haven't been the same since he took off for college."

"I know," Marcy nodded. "I wish he was home, too. And Steve," she added.

"Mad as I used to get at the big lug," Rosemary went on talking about Ken, "we used to have terrific times together. He's quite a guy, your brother."

"I think so, too," Marcy admitted, smiling. "But we could be prejudiced."

"You can say that again." Beneath her red-gold bangs Rosemary's eyes looked very bright, almost as though there might be the sheen of unshed tears added to their usual luster. She took a couple of brooding sips of her drink. "In between scraps, I was pretty crazy about him, I tell you."

"I never knew you scrapped a lot," Marcy said.

"Ken and I?" Rosemary smiled reminiscently. "We were always at it. The thing was," she lowered her voice confidentially although in the cheerful din about them it would have been hard for anyone to overhear, "Ken never wanted to go steady, or anything even close to it. He likes to play the field, although he did date me more than anyone else. But it used to burn me up when he went out with other girls. Now—" Rosemary's tone held a note of regret, "I sort of wish I'd followed his example. If I'd kept a few irons in the fire myself, maybe I wouldn't miss him the way I do."

Before Marcy could answer, Donna Hepple, another of the "widows" asked, "Are you two finished? Let's get out of here. This place gives me the creeps without a man in tow. I mean I feel so conspicuous!"

"I just feel jealous," Jen Blair admitted wistfully.

"After this," Rosemary said, setting her empty glass on the counter, "let's have our after-game refreshments at home!"

Marcy's parents were still up when she came in. This in itself wasn't surprising, since it was only ten-thirty. The strange angle was that they weren't playing cards, or reading, or listening to records. They simply sat there in the living room, not even talking, just staring at the smoldering fire in the fireplace.

"What's the matter?" Marcy asked from the door-way. "You falling asleep in here?"

Mom smiled at her. "We're all talked out, I guess. We've been having quite a lengthy discussion."

There was something a little hesitant about Lila Rhodes' tone, some uncertainty, making Marcy wonder.

"Come here, baby," Dad patted the couch beside him. "There's something we want to tell you."

Dad sounded serious, but not disturbed in the sense he would have been if there were bad news from Ken, or anything like that. Marcy crossed the room to sit beside him, her curiosity mounting.

"What do you want to tell me?" she asked.

"Dear, I don't know how you're going to take this—" Mom began in a breathless little rush altogether unlike her usually calm manner and then her voice sort of ran down.

Dad spoke quietly, his eyes on Marcy's face, "Your mother's decided to go back to nursing."

Marcy could only sit there, staring blankly from one of her parents to the other, could only ask, her voice rising in surprise, "You mean—regular nursing—every day?"

A faint smile curved Mom's mouth. "Not quite," she said. "I'll have two days off a week. Sunday and another one, probably Wednesday." She reached out to lay her hand over Marcy's and give it a little squeeze. "I hope you won't mind too much. They want me to start at the hospital as soon as I can."

"But—" Marcy began. And stopped. What could she say? It sounded as though everything was all set and decided, as if she had no voice in the matter at all.

Her mother must have sensed her thought. She said, "I don't want you to feel I'm just doing this arbitrarily, without giving you a chance to say what you think. I've felt for such a long time that it's something I should do —you and Dad both know that. But if I hadn't gone in to the hospital and practically committed myself to start work on a definite date—well, I'd probably have just kept on putting it off and feeling ashamed of myself. You do understand," she asked earnestly, "both of you?"

"Sure, we do," Dad said staunchly.

Marcy felt his questioning glance on her as the silence stretched out. "But, Mom," when she finally found words, her voice was unsteady, "what about me? What will I do?"

She knew she sounded selfish and uncooperative, but she couldn't help it. A wall of stubbornness built up in her against this absurd plan of her mother's. How could Mom even consider taking a full-time job, going off to the hospital as if she didn't have all sorts of duties and responsibilities at home?

It isn't fair to Dad, or me, Marcy thought.

And she remembered miserably the way she felt whenever she came in from school and her mother happened to be out. Marcy hated that empty feeling in the house, with no good smell of cooking from the kitchen, no pleasant voice greeting her. The memory of that rainy day when she had huddled in her room in the gloomy dimness, feeling so lonely for Steve, so lost without Ken, washed over her. Now it would be that way all the time, Marcy realized. And she felt herself engulfed in a choking tide of self-pity that pushed her close to tears.

Mom's fingers continued to clasp hers. "You'll have plenty to do," Mom said drily. "The house won't run itself, you know. My working will call for a partnership, a three-way partnership. Dad's willing to make adjustments as far as our amusements, the things we love to do together, are concerned. And you—well, I'm counting on you to take over a lot of my duties here at home."

"But how can I?" Marcy objected. "You know I don't have much time after school. And there's my homework and club meetings and everything."

"You've always helped me some," Mom reminded. "The main difference will be that you'll have to take charge of things now. I've lined up Mildred Tinsley to come once a week and give the house a thorough cleaning."

"She's all I need," Marcy said morosely, "she and

those unconsciously funny things she's always saying—
and the way she never puts the furniture back where it
was."

"She should keep you amused, anyway," Dad said
drily.

And Mom pointed out, "She's a good worker. That's
the main thing."

Both her parents, Marcy realized, were disappointed
in the way she had taken Mom's news. It sounded in
their tones, showed in their faces. But she didn't care.
She couldn't help it. So she hadn't risen to the occasion
very well. So she was unhappy about the whole business.
Why should Mom and Dad expect anything else? How
could they assume she'd be pleased and elated?

She said, her voice a little chokey, "I suppose I am
being a stinker, but, gee—"

"No, you're not." Mom's fingers pressed hers. "I
know it won't be too easy for you. But if we all try our
best to work things out, I know we can manage."

"It's more—that I'll miss you," Marcy admitted, "than
that I'll mind the extra work so much."

"But I'll be home evenings." Mom's smile was gentle.
"And you're so busy now with school activities and your
friends and all, you're not around too much. With all
the extra responsibilities you'll have, there won't be
much chance for you to miss me." She went on, after
a moment's silence, "I wouldn't have considered going
back to work when you were younger. But you're almost
grown up now. And Ken's away."

That was just it, Marcy thought desolately. Ken was
away. Her mother's decision would have been much

easier to face if Ken were still at home. Then there would have been the two of them around after school. It wouldn't have been nearly so bleak. Still, since Mom's mind was made up and everything was all set, she supposed she'd just have to make the best of it.

She managed a faint smile and both her parents looked a bit relieved.

Dad said to Mom, "You'll have time before you start work to give her a good briefing on all the things she'll have to do, won't you? Get her started off right?"

"Of course," Mom nodded. "I thought we'd take all next week to get things organized. I know Marcy can manage. Mainly, there'll be the shopping for food and planning and cooking meals—I can help after I get home, naturally, but I won't be here in time to do everything. If Mildred gives the house a good going over once a week, it shouldn't require much more cleaning. And we'll send the laundry out, except for the most fragile things—"

Marcy listened and nodded as her mother talked on. She answered when a question was asked, even contributed a few comments of her own. But a small, inner part of her mind remained entirely aloof from the discussion.

What else could happen to mess things up for her, Marcy wondered? First there had been Steve's departure, and Ken's. Then Liz's contrary, unreasonable attitude had developed. This long-awaited senior year, of which Marcy had expected so much in the way of interest and stimulating activity, had certainly let her down with a thump. And now, to place the final straw on the growing load of her dissatisfactions, there was her mother's decision to go back to work.

Oh, well, Marcy tried to tell herself, brooding isn't going to help.

Still, she had the feeling that she'd be spending a good part of her time brooding from now on . . .

❧ SEVEN ❧

Marcy Manages

MARCY WASN'T QUITE SURE HOW TO GO about telling Liz the news. Should she really unburden herself, or try to conceal how bad she actually felt over Mom's decision? Such hesitation on Marcy's part would have been inconceivable a while back. But lately she hadn't felt so close to Liz, as sure of her understanding and sympathy. Ever since their sharp disagreement over "The Widows," Marcy had sensed some change in her friend. This perverse new Liz, she suspected, might be quite capable of taking Mom's view of things, of considering Marcy's true attitude childish and unreasonable.

And so when she and Liz were walking over to the library that Saturday morning, Marcy began by simply laying the bare facts before her. "Guess what! My mother's decided to go back to nursing. She's starting at the hospital next week."

"You're kidding!" Liz accused, obviously surprised. Then, when Marcy had added a few more details, she shook her head wonderingly and said, "Well, you're certainly a lot more philosophical about it than I'd be! The mere idea of having all that housework and stuff dumped on my shoulders would give me the screaming meemies!"

Marcy grinned at her. Apparently Liz wasn't as drastically changed as she had feared. She went on to confide in her further as to the way she really felt about the whole thing. "It isn't," Marcy finished, "that I'm not proud of Mom. She feels she should go back to nursing, so she's doing it. But I don't know how I'm going to manage."

Liz nodded sympathetically. "Oh, I think your mother's wonderful, too. But there's no question about it being pretty rough on you. Even with a cleaning woman—" she broke off with a little dubious shrug.

"Mildred's a character," Marcy said. "The things she comes out with! Like calling that new chair of ours oliver green. And once she told Mom about a friend of hers who had ammonia and had to be put in an Oxydol tent."

Liz laughed, "Like that Mrs. Malaprop in the play of Sheridan's we read in English."

Somehow, Marcy felt a little better about the whole thing after she'd talked with Liz. Not much, but a little. Writing to Steve about it helped some, too.

She managed to keep her letter in a drily humorous vein. At least, it was some news to pass along. Marcy couldn't help feeling that her recent letters to Steve had been a little thin. The sad truth, which she wouldn't have dreamed of admitting to him, was that nothing much was happening to her since he went away. The letter she wrote about her mother, and all the changes in store for Marcy herself, was one of the longest and most interesting she had sent him.

Steve wrote back: "I think you're pretty wonderful, taking over for your mother at home, so she can go back to nursing. A lot of girls would be griping to high heaven. Even if it's kind of tough for you, think of all the stuff you'll learn about how to run a house. Might come in handy later on."

Marcy felt a warm little glow over Steve's words of approval. And even Ken broke down and wrote her a couple of heartening lines on a picture postcard. "I'm proud of you, kid. Just be sure you learn to cook before I get back."

If she didn't, Marcy thought a shade grimly, it wouldn't be for lack of practice.

In one way things weren't so bad after her mother went back to work as Marcy had expected. In another they were worse. The actual housework didn't prove too time-consuming. Beds and dishes and marketing soon fell into a sort of routine. Mom was home to help evenings and Dad pitched in, too. Of course, his idea of assistance usually consisted of broiling steaks or concocting a special kind of hamburgers that were his pride and joy, but even though he left the kitchen a shambles, his intentions were good. Marcy was forever cutting her fingers peeling vegetables or burning her knuckles on the oven.

She told Liz drily, "It's getting so I don't feel fully dressed without a strip of adhesive tape somewhere or other."

Still, all this Marcy found she could take in her stride. The thing that got her was the loneliness. No matter how much work there might be for her to do after school, the house's silence and emptiness seemed to wrap her about like a chill garment as soon as she came in. She would go around switching on lamps against the encroaching dusk, turning on the radio for company. Liz often stopped in with her for a little while.

"I don't blame you for hating to come in all alone," Liz sympathized. "An empty house gives me the creeps, too. You know you're always welcome to come home with me."

"But there's work I should do here," Marcy reminded her. "I never have time to straighten up the house mornings. And I have to get dinner started. I guess I'll just have to learn to be more self-sufficient."

"Yeah," Liz agreed rather doubtfully. "I guess so."

One day when Marcy came in alone after school and was feeling especially forlorn, she checked up on the kitchen calendar to see just how long it was until Thanksgiving. Almost six weeks, she thought with dismay. Still, if you called it thirty-nine days, it didn't sound so bad. In thirty-nine days, she told herself, Steve would be home. Her heart lifted crazily at the thought. She had known when he left that she would miss him, but she hadn't realized how much. Fond of him as she was, she hadn't expected to be counting the days till his return.

And probably she wouldn't be doing that if she were having much fun. But she hadn't had a single real date since Steve went to college. Oh, she'd had a few Cokes with Bix, or someone equally unimportant in her scheme of things. She'd gone to games and other school activities with Rosemary and the rest of "The Widows." But so far as having a boy ask her to go out with him—well, it just hadn't happened. Nor was it likely to, Marcy thought glumly.

True, there wasn't anyone around with whom she was anxious to have dates, still life was rather dull without them. Liz seemed quite content with her tall Hank Novak. But Marcy didn't envy her. It was all very well for Liz to point out that at least Hank was here at hand, that he was really very interesting when you got to know him. Liz was entitled to her opinion, and Marcy was entitled to hers. And in Marcy's opinion Hank wasn't nearly as attractive as Steve. No one she could think of compared with Steve. She hadn't, she felt, fully appreciated him when he was around, hadn't realized how wonderful he was. She had actually taken him for granted at times, incredible as such conduct now seemed. His absence had sharpened and intensified her feelings toward him.

In thirty-nine days, Marcy repeated rather breathlessly to herself, Steve would be home again. There was the long four-day week end to look forward to. How was she ever going to bear to wait?

Maybe, Marcy thought wistfully, Steve was as lost without her as she was without him. Boys never liked to break down and admit anything like that. She knew that much from her brother. But although Steve's letters always sounded rushed and busy, he never wrote anything about other girls. Maybe he wasn't dating anyone, either. Marcy's heart beat faster at the thought. Maybe he was missing her dreadfully, too . . .

Liz tried to talk Marcy into going on a double date

with her and Hank. "I'm sure we can line up someone for you."

But Marcy shook her head. "Oh, I don't think so, Liz. Thanks just the same, though."

Liz frowned at her. They were walking down the corridor at school, on their way from morning study hall to their next class. "I can't understand you lately," Liz said. "You seem determined not to have any fun at all."

Marcy shook her head. "No, I'm not. But—I might as well wait till Steve's home now. It's almost Thanksgiving."

"You're crazy," Liz accused flatly. "That's weeks off yet."

"Only a few," Marcy murmured dreamily.

"I'm surprised you haven't counted up the hours and minutes." Liz's tone dripped sarcasm. "Honestly!"

Marcy smiled at her. "So long as I'm not complaining—"

"But you should be," Liz broke in. "That's just the point. You should be griping like crazy over not having any dates, or else you should start doing something constructive about it." They had reached the point where their paths parted. But before she turned to go, Liz admitted, "I know it's none of my business, but I hate to see you acting so silly!"

Poor Liz, Marcy thought forbearingly as she watched her friend stalk away. She meant well, but she just didn't understand. If Liz couldn't have one man, she'd settle for another. She simply couldn't grasp Marcy's reasons for preferring to wait for Steve rather than accept some wholly unsatisfactory substitute.

Marcy discovered a few nights later that her parents, too, were beginning to worry about her.

It was one of those dismal fall evenings when it was good to be in-doors. Sleety rain lashed at the windows. Mom, whose feet were usually tired from being on them most of the day, was stretched out comfortably on the couch in housecoat and slippers. Dad had just poked up the smoldering logs in the fireplace and put a selection of classical records on the player. Muted music covered the sound of the wind and rain and it was very cozy there in the Rhodes' living room. Marcy, who had done her homework earlier, leafed contentedly through the pages of a new magazine.

And then, without any advance warning, Dad cleared his throat purposefully and said, "It seems to me you're spending an awful lot of evenings at home, Marcy."

She lifted accusing dark eyes to her father's face, but before she could answer, her mother said, "We do so want you to have a wonderful time your senior year, dear. Ken had such fun. He was on the go so much we actually worried a little over him. But you—" Mom left it at that.

Marcy could tell from their manner that they'd talked it all over and decided to try to find out what was the matter. If that wasn't just like parents, she thought in annoyance. When you chased around too much they worried over your health and your school work. But if you didn't go out enough, that bothered them, too.

She asked, her tone good-naturedly casual, "What's the matter? Getting tired of the sight of me?"

"No, of course not," Mom said and her blue eyes were troubled. "The thing is, I'd hate to think my working is spoiling things for you. I know your time after school is pretty well taken up with all the extra jobs you've had dumped on you. But you must never feel you can't go out evenings if you want to."

"Oh, I know that," Marcy told her.

Dad put in, frowning, "There's just one point I'd like to get straight. You and Steve Judson—you didn't make any crazy promise not to go out with other people while he's away?"

"No, we didn't," Marcy said honestly. "We talked it over and both of us thought it wouldn't be sensible to figure we were going steady while Steve's at college."

"Well, I'm glad to hear that," Dad said with relief. "You're both far too young to—" he broke off, staring at her questioningly. "But if you decided you would go out with other boys, why aren't you doing it?"

Marcy shrugged. "Oh, I don't know. I suppose I would if anyone I was interested in asked me. But this year's seniors aren't anything to raise a girl's blood pressure."

Dad seemed satisfied, but Mom asked, her almost too penetrating gaze squarely on Marcy, "How is Liz coping with the problem?"

Marcy said rather shortly, "Liz isn't very hard to suit. Anyway," she added before her mother could say anything more, "do we have to get into a hassle about it right now? Steve will be home for Thanksgiving in a couple of weeks and I'll have more dates than I know what to do with."

Both her parents smiled at her, letting the matter drop. Marcy knew they only wanted her to be happy.

She managed to keep busy enough the next few weeks,

so that Mom and Dad didn't worry about her not having any fun. She worked on the decorations committee for the Fall Dance and felt a small qualm of self-pity to see the school gym transformed into a white-and-silver fairyland and know that she would have no part in the festivities to follow. But, she told herself, she'd been to a lot of dances. Missing one wouldn't kill her.

As Thanksgiving actually drew near, Marcy's anticipation mounted to a dizzy pitch. Steve had written— how well she knew the words by heart!—"Tell your new men they'll have to step aside next week end. The ol' maestro's coming home and he intends to take over." The fact that there weren't any "new men" to tell only served to make things simpler, Marcy thought.

She had her soft dark hair set in a new way and did her nails till they were perfect. She experimented with various shades of lipstick. And all the while her heart kept hurrying each time the thought, "Steve's coming!" flashed through her mind.

She found she could scarcely remember how he looked. His graduation picture, which she had framed on her dressing table, kept superimposing itself between her and the memory of Steve's face. But one thing she was sure of. She was going to be the happiest girl in Westfield during those four enchanted days when Steve was home. She was looking forward to seeing Ken, too, of course. But not in the same way. Not nearly in the same way.

Mom told her on Monday, her tone apologetic, "You realize I'm going to have to work on Thanksgiving, don't you?"

"Work?" Marcy stared at her blankly. "But it's a holiday!"

"Hospitals must run just the same," her mother reminded her. "Sick people have to be taken care of. And my day off is Wednesday, not Thursday."

"You mean," Marcy asked, appalled, "I'll have to get the dinner?"

Mom smiled sympathetically. "I'm afraid so, honey. I sort of felt Dad out about eating out. But he hated the idea. On Thanksgiving, of all days. It's such a homey, family sort of holiday. And I know Ken will feel the same. But it won't really be so bad for you. My being home the day before will give us the chance to get a lot of the food ready ahead of time. I'll bake the pie and mix the stuffing. Of course, you'll have to put it in the turkey the next day, but that's not much of a job. And if we fix a gelatin salad and I get the rolls all set—" she broke off to ask, "You do think you can manage, don't you?"

Marcy nodded. Mom sounded so sorry, she just couldn't let her down. Marcy said, "Sure, I can manage. And we won't eat our big dinner till evening, so you can be home, too. It just wouldn't seem like Thanksgiving without you."

Mom put her arm around Marcy and gave her a quick hug. "I'm really awfully proud of you, the way you've taken over. Dad is, too."

Marcy smiled at her. "Don't go trying to bribe me with compliments now. It'll get you nowhere."

Mom laughed. "Ken will be around to help some, too," she remembered. "Or maybe you won't consider his efforts very helpful. But he and Dad—well, they mean well. It's just that men are so messy in a kitchen!"

Marcy didn't answer. She was lost in a lovely dream. When Ken was around, Steve would be around, too, since they were taking the night train back together on Wednesday. Steve would have to spend some time with his parents, of course. Marcy realized that. Still, he'd be with her as much as he possibly could. She didn't doubt that for a minute.

Steve, her heart whispered. Steve.

Luckily, the things Mom was saying weren't too vital, because Marcy didn't hear one further word.

EIGHT

The New Steve

AT THE LAST MINUTE THERE WAS A SWITCH in Steve's and Ken's plans. Ken phoned, reversing the charges, of course, to tell his family that no one need meet the midnight train in Clay City, after all. A fraternity brother would be driving right through Westfield on his way home, so Steve and Ken would ride with him.

"Splitting the gas three ways will be a lot cheaper than train fare," Ken pointed out. "It'll be better all around. The only thing is, we may be later getting in. Don't wait up for me. Just leave the door unlocked and there I'll be Thanksgiving morning."

Marcy, who had planned to drive over to Clay City with her parents, couldn't help feeling just a little let down. Now she wouldn't get to see Steve until Thursday. But Dad, who didn't relish driving in heavy city traffic, was relieved. And Mom said, "I won't have to be up so late this way. Seems as though that old alarm rings earlier every morning."

When Marcy got home from school on Wednesday, it was like old times. There were sounds of activity in the kitchen and lovely spicy smells in the air. She put her books down happily, flung aside her coat, and went out to join Mom.

"What can I do to help?" Marcy asked.

Mom smiled at her. "Well, let's see. Oh, you might add the fruit to the salad now. I think the gelatine's solid enough." She went on, "I don't think there'll be too much left for you tomorrow. The pies are baked and the stuffing's all made. The rolls are ready except for baking them tomorrow."

Marcy assured her, as she went about preparing the salad, "I'll manage perfectly all right. Don't you worry. You didn't even need to do so much."

Mom said, "I want you to have some free time, though. After all, you've been looking forward to this week end a long time."

Marcy smiled, feeling happiness curl around her heart. "Gee, it just doesn't seem possible Ken will be home tomorrow, does it?"

Mom's tone was teasing. "Ken—or Steve?"

"Both," Marcy said and their glances met in a long understanding look, as they laughed together . . .

Marcy had felt sure she'd wake up very early on Thanksgiving. But her parents' alarm clock didn't disturb her, or the sounds of her mother departing for the hospital. It was almost ten when Marcy's sleepy glance first sought the little clock on her bedside table. Ten, Marcy thought, appalled? It couldn't be! But the clock was running and bright sunshine lay in a band across her bed.

Marcy thrust aside the covers and jumped out. The shag rug tickled the soles of her bare feet, but she was scarcely aware of the sensation. She slid into her terry-cloth robe and knotted the belt firmly as she sped down the hall to Ken's room, fully expecting to find him still sleeping.

Nor was she disappointed. There was Ken, sprawled kitty-cornered across the bed, face-downward on the pillow. His toast-colored hair was sticking up in points, one shoulder was hunched defensively against the sunshine pouring in his window.

"Ken!" Marcy yelled at him and swooped across the room, avoiding the opened suitcase on the floor, to land on the foot of the bed with a thump.

Ken said something unintelligible that came out in a kind of growl and burrowed deeper. But Marcy laid firm hands on his shoulder and shook. "Wake up!" she commanded. "You're home, remember? It's me, Marcy."

"I'd have known that," Ken moaned, turning his head slightly so that he could look at her out of one reproachful eye. "Nobody but you ever jumps on my bed and starts manhandling me when it's hardly even daylight yet and I didn't get in till two."

He shifted position still further then and Marcy saw his grin. Sitting up, he reached out and gave her a bear hug, then held her off by both shoulders and took a good look at her. "Loopy as ever," he said regretfully.

"Why?" Marcy demanded. "Because I woke you up?"

Ken shook his head. "Barging into a guy's room like that, any guy's room, even your brother's. Your hair's a mess and your robe's strictly from hunger and—"

Marcy interrupted, glaring, "I thought you might have improved, but you're the same old stinker! What do you expect, glamour the first thing in the morning?"

"First impressions," Ken informed her, a teasing glint in his blue eyes, "are so important! You haven't got any lipstick on, either."

"I practically never sleep in it," Marcy said scathingly. "You're no picture yourself, you know." She reached out and mussed his hair still more and, in finishing, gave it an intentional hard yank.

"Ouch!" Ken growled. "Why, you little—"

Squealing, Marcy felt herself hawled over onto her brother's lap. He proceeded to spank her heartily on the spot provided by nature for such punishment.

But suddenly she stopped squealing and Ken's hand was arrested in mid-air by the mellow sound of the doorbell chiming. After a second Marcy heard her father's footsteps as he went to answer it.

"Who on earth—?" her questioning glance sought Ken's as he let her go.

"Steve," her brother informed her with a smug and infuriating air of satisfaction.

Marcy's eyes widened in shocked horror. "Oh, no!"

Steve couldn't be here yet. Not when she wasn't ready to see him. Not after all her planning as to just what she was going to wear. Marcy clutched her old robe more tightly about her and she scrambled off Ken's bed. From downstairs she could hear her father's pleased greeting as he invited Steve in.

"Oh, yes," Ken said, a wicked gleam in his eye. "And if I know Steve, he'll be up here to rout me out as soon as he hears I'm not up yet. There is nothing," Ken's voice pursued Marcy as she sprinted desperately for the shelter of her own room, "that a Beta Zeta likes better than a chance to drag a hapless brother from his slumbers. We even have a secret and horrible method of doing it, known as the B Z Treatment. You should hear the screams of the anguished victims as—"

Marcy shut her door hard and leaned against it, panting. That would be all she needed, she thought, for Steve to come upstairs in search of Ken and catch her in his room looking like this! Ken might be kidding her, but she hadn't dared gamble on it. Still, as moments passed and there was no sound of footsteps on the stairs, but only the pleasant hum of Steve's conversation with her father, Marcy began to think this might be the case.

She gathered up her clothes and sneaked into the bathroom, pausing only to hiss, "You louse!" through her brother's door. Ken did not answer. He had apparently gone back to sleep.

Marcy took a quick shower, hurriedly dressed in her brown corduroy skirt and lemon-yellow sweater, and brushed her hair till it shone. If only Steve liked her new hair do. If only he still liked her!

Marcy's insides were a quivering mass of hope and uncertainty as she went down the carpeted stairs. Quietly she pursued the sound of voices along the hallway, wanting one glimpse of Steve before he saw her. When she reached the kitchen door, there he was, sitting with his back toward her, having a companionable cup of coffee with her father. In the second before her father said, "Here's Marcy," she noted that Steve's dark hair was cut shorter than she had ever seen it and that his shoulders, in a gray-and-white plaid flannel shirt, seemed wider than she had remembered.

Then Steve was on his feet, grinning down at her, exclaiming, "It's about time!"

His hands reached out and pulled her close to him and his lips met hers in a short kiss that made Marcy's pulse pound and sent hot color to her cheeks. Never before had Steve kissed her in front of her father. The Steve who had left for college in September wouldn't have dared.

But Dad only grinned and shook his head when Steve said to him, "I hope you don't mind, Mr. Rhodes. I've missed your daughter." He held her off then and feasted his eyes on her for a long minute. "What," he asked then, "are you all dressed up for?"

Marcy answered, with a little shaken laugh, "What did you expect, blue jeans and a tee shirt?"

"Isn't that what you still usually wear around home in the morning?" Steve queried.

"It certainly is," Dad put in drily. "She must have heard you come."

"So?" Marcy quoted Ken, "First impressions are so important!"

Steve chuckled, pulling out a chair for Marcy politely, then sitting down beside her. "My first impression of you goes back a long way. You were about twelve and you still had braces on your teeth and you were always getting in the way when Ken and I had big deals going on."

"I know," Marcy said, "I was just Ken's kid sister and a pesty nuisance."

"Oh, not so pesty," Steve said, his dark eyes on her

face. "It was just that I was too young to appreciate girls."

Did he really seem older than he had in September, Marcy wondered as they talked on. Or did she merely imagine it? He wasn't quite so handsome as she had remembered him. But that could be due to his butch haircut. Or it could be that she had let her imagination build up a better-than-reality mental image of him, because she missed him so.

After a few minutes Dad murmured something about wanting to catch a news broadcast and faded out of the room almost imperceptibly. Good old Dad, Marcy thought gratefully. Apparently Steve appreciated his thoughtfulness, too.

"Tactful man, your father," he grinned, capturing Marcy's fingers and holding them close.

Marcy smiled and nodded. But her fingers didn't feel entirely at home in Steve's grasp. Some strangeness she couldn't fathom seemed to drift between them like mist. Did Steve sense it, too, she wondered?

Rather oddly, their talk was less easy than it had been with her father there. Silences fell upon them, not the cozy silences of companionable understanding, but the kind you felt constrained in and anxious to think of something—anything—to say. Self-consciousness, such as she hadn't suffered in Steve's presence in years, dragged at Marcy. Maybe, she thought, he didn't even want to hold her hand, but was just doing so because he thought she expected it.

With the murmured excuse that she was starved and wanted to round up some breakfast, she pulled her hand from Steve's and went around the kitchen, gathering up food. She came back to the table with a glass of fruit juice, a couple of sweet rolls and a cup of coffee.

"Like some more?" she asked Steve, the percolator poised over his cup.

"Sure," Steve said. "I'll have one of those rolls, too, if you don't mind." He gestured toward Marcy's cup.

"Since when? You never used to like coffee."

She still didn't, if the truth were told. But it seemed so babyish to sit drinking milk with Steve taking coffee.

"Oh, I drink it sometimes," Marcy said, stirring in cream till the contents of her cup assumed a pale beige color, and adding a couple of spoonsful of sugar. "You never used to like it, either," she pointed out.

"I got educated around the fraternity house," Steve chuckled. "The brothers drink gallons of it."

He started talking about college then, telling Marcy of places she hadn't seen, people she didn't know, experiences in which she had no part. She sat listening, feeling stupid and quiet, nibbling at her sweet roll and trying to down her coffee.

After a few minutes, Steve said apologetically. "But this isn't very interesting to you, is it, Marce?"

"Oh, yes," Marcy assured him, "Yes, of course, it is."

Steve's grin was as appealing as ever. "Don't hand me that. So the modern history professor is a stuffed shirt and the new Student Union has bowling alleys in the basement—what's that to you? Tell me," he demanded, "about high school and what all you've been doing."

Marcy felt a crazy impulse to burst into hysterical laughter. Steve probably had no idea how much he sounded like an adult trying to make conversation with a child, querying politely, "How is everything going at school?" Maybe he didn't mean to sound that way at all, but he did. And his attitude, unconscious though it might be, made Marcy feel even more ill at ease and shut away from him than before.

She murmured, "Oh, everything's just the same there. And I haven't done anything special.

How scintillating, Marcy thought! That should kill the conversation entirely. And her words weren't even true. Things weren't the same at school. Not the same, at all! The fun and excitement of last year, when Steve had been around, had shriveled up and disappeared. Only the last part of her statement had been factual. She certainly hadn't been doing anything special.

"I don't suppose," Steve was saying, "you have much time, with your mother working. But you still must have your evenings free for dates. You can level with me, you know. I won't hold it against you. So long as your new men realize I've got priority while I'm home and don't get in my way—"

"Hi, you two," Ken's voice broke in as he came galumphing down the stairs. "I've given you all the time to yourselves I'm going to. What's for breakfast? I'm starving!"

Never, Marcy felt gratefully, had an interruption been more timely. In another second, she might have been forced into the degrading admission that she hadn't had a single date since Steve's departure for college, that there wasn't even one new man in her life who'd have to step aside for him.

Good old Ken, Marcy thought, jumping up eagerly to wait on him. She must remember to do something perfectly wonderful for him sometime . . .

❧ NINE ❧

The Quarrel

MARCY FIXED KEN'S BREAKFAST, PORK SAU-
sage and scrambled eggs, sweet rolls and marmalade,
fruit juice and coffee and milk. "Save a little room for
turkey," she warned him, laughing.

"That'll be hours yet," Ken said. "We aren't going to
eat till Mom gets home at six, are we? I'll probably need
a couple more meals before then."

"You won't get them from me," Marcy informed him.
"From now on till dinner, you're on your own. What's
the matter? Don't they feed you at that fraternity
house?"

"Oh, sure," Ken said, digging into his breakfast enthusiastically. "We've got the best cook on campus,
wouldn't you say, Steve?"

Steve nodded. "We sure have. All the other houses
try to snitch her away from us, but she's true to good ol'
Beta Zeta."

As conversation flowed on between the two boys,

Marcy listened and tried to take part. But the incidents they recounted, while interesting in themselves, were completely alien to her. What did she know about college politics and which professors were good joes? Or about fraternity rushing and Hell Week and bull sessions and so on? During the course of the talk Ken mentioned several girls, particularly one named Lee Creighton, who, it seemed, must have been taking up a good deal of his free time. Steve, Marcy noted with interest, had nothing to say about any girls at all. But once when Ken spoke of someone with the intriguing name of Thea, he stopped rather abruptly and with a pained expression. Marcy strongly suspected that Steve might have kicked him under the table. She filed Thea away in her memory, for future investigation. And her feeling of disappointment, of being left out, grew until it ached in her throat and made her more and more silent.

Finally Steve said, his eyes on her face, "I don't think all this stuff is very interesting to Marcy. Quit yakking about college, Ken, and let's find out what's been going on at home. Come on, Marce, bring us up to date."

But Marcy said, "I've told you everything in my letters. Nothing much has been happening, really." She got to her feet and moved purposefully toward the refrigerator. "Besides, I've got a Thanksgiving dinner to cook. I have to get the turkey in the oven hours ahead of time."

"Can't we help?" Steve offered.

"Careful there, boy," Ken told him. "She might take you up on that."

"I don't know just what you could do," Marcy smiled at Steve. "Had any experience stuffing a turkey?"

"Well, no," Steve admitted. "Stuffing myself with turkey is more in my line. And speaking of that, what time is it getting to be?"

"Almost one," Ken said and Marcy glanced at the kitchen clock in amazement. Where had the time gone? They'd been sitting around talking for hours. And she had so many things to do and a turkey as big as the one they had would take forever to cook. Mom had warned her particularly to get it in in plenty of time.

"I've got to get busy," Marcy said firmly.

She opened the refrigerator door and began struggling to take the turkey out.

"Here, let me help," Steve said, jumping to his feet.

He pulled the bird in its waxed paper wrapping out and stood there, holding it gingerly.

"Put it here on the sink," Marcy instructed.

She turned from the refrigerator with the big mixing bowl full of bread stuffing in her hands. "I guess I'd better light the oven first, so it'll be heating."

"How domestic," Ken murmured, leaning his chin on his palm to regard her with mock admiration. "I never knew my little sister had it in her."

"If you don't shush," Marcy warned him, "you'll get this stuffing on your head."

"Quit heckling her," Steve told Ken good-humoredly. "Can't you see she's got work to do?"

As Marcy spooned stuffing into the enormous yawning cavern of the turkey, the two boys hovered close about, getting in her way as they watched and making silly suggestions. If she had felt more sure of herself, it probably wouldn't have bothered her so much. But this was the first time Marcy had ever prepared a turkey for roasting and she felt increasingly hot and self-conscious and resentful. It was all very well for them to joke about her awkwardness, they didn't have the responsibility of getting the meal ready. Marcy's hair fell forward into her eyes and she brushed at it with the back of one hand. She probably looked a perfect mess, she thought desperately. Of all the un-glamorous occupations for Steve to see her at! Probably he had never observed the mysterious-sounding Thea at college doing anything more utilitarian than carrying a couple of books from one class to another. At that moment, Marcy hated Thea.

She actually felt relieved when Steve finally said, "Gee, I'm afraid I'll have to get home now. We're having dinner at two and the house is going to be crawling with relatives. And I'll have to stick around till evening."

He sounded so disappointed, so like the old Steve, that Marcy couldn't help smiling at him. "I'm glad you got over for a little while," she told him, although it wasn't entirely true. In a way, she thought, it might have been better if he hadn't got to see her until later, until she was through with all her tasks and able to really concentrate on him.

"How about tonight?" Steve asked. "Could we go out for a while?"

Marcy nodded. "Of course. I'd love to."

Steve squeezed her hand hard for a minute, looking deep into her eyes. "Around eight? I can get away by then."

"So can I," Marcy told him.

Curiously, he still seemed rather like a stranger to her. But not quite so much so as he had at first. And tonight, Marcy told herself, it would be better, much better.

Without Ken around, or her father, without a lot of cooking hanging over her, it would be altogether different.

Steve and she would have a chance to get acquainted all over again . . .

Marcy burned her wrist on the oven door and couldn't get quite all the lumps out of the mashed potatoes. She spilled a bottle of milk all over the kitchen floor. But Ken and Dad helped mop it up. And, sensing that she was on the verge of tears, they didn't even kid her. Aside from these and a few other minor disasters, Marcy's first Thanksgiving dinner was quite a success. And it was such fun for the whole family to be together again, talking and laughing around the table with its green damask cloth and tall silver candlesticks, that Marcy almost man aged to forget the pain of her burn and the annoyance of all the accumulated trials that had messed up her day.

Mom told Marcy, as they were finishing their pumpkin pie, "I think it's just wonderful, the way you took hold and did everything. Now I'll do the dishes and clearing up."

"Not alone," Dad said firmly. "You worked all day, too. I'll help. We aren't due over at the Kendalls' for a couple of hours. We've got plenty of time."

"I'll help, too," Ken offered magnanimously. "Let Marcy go and make herself beautiful for Steve. She looks kind of done in, poor kid."

"You've got a date, too," Marcy demurred halfheartedly.

Ken said, "I'm all ready, though. And Rosemary isn't expecting me till eight."

"Okay." Marcy grinned at him and her parents. "You twisted my arm."

After a warm shower and a brisk rubdown, she felt better. She dressed carefully in a skirt of soft red wool and a matching jersey blouse that Steve hadn't even seen yet. She spent several minutes deciding which medallion to wear. When she was ready at last, she knew Steve had been waiting for her a good ten minutes. But the result was worth it, Marcy thought, turning this way and that in front of her mirror. She doubted that Thea whatever-the-rest-of-her-name-was looked any better when she went out with Steve. At least, she hoped she didn't. Once again dislike of the unknown Thea nibbled at Marcy.

When the front door had shut behind them and they were walking down the drive to Steve's car, he said, "Well, finally! I thought I was never going to get you to myself."

Marcy's voice wasn't too steady, admitting, "Neither did I."

He held the car door open for her, then went around and slid in beside her. Marcy felt his arm around her shoulders pulling her close. Their lips met and clung for a moment and excitement exploded like shooting stars in Marcy's blood stream. Being kissed after almost a three-months interval was a heady business—as unsettling as being kissed for the very first time, she thought.

Starting the car a moment later, Steve fumbled a little with the ignition switch and his voice was husky saying, "Gee, Marce, I've missed you."

"Me, too," Marcy admitted.

Conversation with Steve was easier now than it had

been this morning. They drove around and talked and talked, as though they couldn't catch up on all the things they had to say to each other.

Finally Steve said, his tone apologetic, "Maybe you wanted to go somewhere, a movie or something. I didn't even think to ask."

Marcy smiled, murmuring, "We can go to a movie anytime. Tonight I just feel like getting to know you again. It was—funny this morning—"

"Yeah," Steve nodded. "I know. It was almost as if we were strangers. I was kind of worried."

So he had felt it, too. It hadn't just been her notion. He had felt it and had been troubled by it. Somehow the realization made them seem closer than ever.

Marcy said, "It's queer why we should feel that way, as well as we know each other. And, after all, you've only been gone a few months."

"Yeah," Steve agreed, "but you were gone a lot of this summer. And then right after you came back from Colorado, I had to leave."

Marcy said, "And even though we wrote a lot—well, letters just aren't the same."

"Yours certainly aren't," Steve agreed. "You never seemed to tell me anything. Why, do you know, I don't think you mentioned having a single date, all the time I've been gone. And, of course, I know you were going out with other guys and the fact that you didn't mention any of them—well, it seemed sort of like you were holding out on me."

"You didn't mention any dates, either," Marcy pointed out.

"Sure, I did," Steve denied. "I told you about the

Freshman Mixer and going to the Union to bowl and—"

"But you didn't mention any special girl," Marcy broke in. "You didn't mention—" she paused for a second, then said the name aloud resolutely, "Thea."

Steve gave her a brief startled glance, before turning his attention back to the road ahead. "Who told you about Thea?"

"Nobody," Marcy admitted, making little pleats in the fabric of her skirt with thumb and forefinger. "I just heard her name come up in your and Ken's conversation this morning."

"I didn't even realize we mentioned her," Steve said rather crossly. "She's just a girl at college, a freshman."

"I think her name's pretty," Marcy admitted. "What's the rest of it."

"Cunningham," Steve said. "Would you like to stop by the Sweet Shop and—"

"Thea Cunningham," Marcy repeated thoughtfully. "She sounds—oh, small, I should say, with blond hair and big blue eyes and—"

"She's tall and has brown eyes and her hair's cut that sort of crazy Italian way, kind of chewed off, but on her it doesn't look too bad because—"

"My," Marcy interrupted, "you must have studied her *very* carefully. Have you been dating her a lot?"

"No," Steve said and his voice sounded unhappy, "only a few times, actually. And I didn't study her carefully—you just seemed anxious to know what she looked like, so I told you."

"Why," Marcy asked airily, "should I care how she looks? But if you're so mad for her you want to talk about her all the time, of course, I'll listen."

"Look!" Steve exploded. "I don't want to talk about her. You're the one who dragged her into the conversation! But I don't see why you care if I took her out for a few times. We agreed before I left that we'd both have dates with other people. You know we did, Marce. And I'm not holding it against you.

Marcy felt anger boil up in her like a geyser getting ready to erupt. Maybe she was being unreasonable. Maybe it wasn't really anger at Steve at all. Perhaps it was simply the end result of all her weeks of anticipation, of her own lack of fun and dates, of the extra hateful tasks she'd had to assume lately, of the general dullness of her life with Steve gone. Whatever it was and whatever its basis, the effect was the same.

Words poured from Marcy's mouth, furious, resentful words. She told Steve just what she thought of him. She accused him of pretending to like her and sneaking behind her back to date another girl. She called him fickle and said he had deceived her.

No man could take such an outburst without trying to defend himself. But everything Steve said only made Marcy more angry. The final blow was his reiterated statement that she had no right to get sore at him. She hadn't confided in him about her other dates, either. This Marcy couldn't deny. Because to deny it was to admit to Steve the degrading fact that she hadn't had any other dates, that she hadn't gone out with another boy since his departure.

The upshot was that Marcy insisted on being taken home at once. And Steve, tight-lipped and glaring, complied with her demand. They parted wordlessly, with only the hard slam of the car door, the sharp tap of

Marcy's heels on the walk, to break the silence. Steve shifted gears with a noisy jerk, backed the car down the drive and left. The diminishing hum of the motor was the only sound in the still night.

The complete emptiness of the house reached out and laid clammy hands on Marcy as soon as she had shut the front door behind her. Mom and Dad, she remembered, had gone over to the Kendalls for the evening. Ken had a date with Rosemary. No one would be home for hours. She was all alone.

Suddenly Marcy began to cry, out loud, as she hadn't cried in years. Tears streamed down her face and sobs shook her. But what difference did it make? There was no one to hear and be disturbed, to feel sorry for her. No one at all . . .

❦ TEN ❦

Blue Friday

MARCY'S PARENTS HAD LEFT FOR THEIR RE-
spective jobs before she got up the next morning. Ken
was still asleep, but today Marcy didn't go barging into
his room. Instead she dressed as quietly as possible, not
wanting to disturb him. She examined her face critically
in the merciless fluorescent lights in the bathroom, but
no visible traces of last night's tears remained to embar-
rass her. That was a break, anyway.

She went lackadaisically down the stairs and out to the
kitchen. Was it only yesterday morning she had sat here,
talking with Steve, feeling the warm pressure of his hand
on hers? Sunshine splashed across the table, just as it
had then, but that was the only point of resemblance.
Today the usually cheerful kitchen seemed a shell, a pod
in which Marcy rattled like a lone pea, as she moved
about assembling her solitary meal. She turned the radio
on, quite low, just for company. And—wouldn't you
know?—some disk jockey was spinning a sentimental

tune she and Steve had danced to countless times last spring.

I don't care! Marcy thought.

She took a spoonful of cereal stoically, forcing it down, although it seemed flat and tasteless. She wouldn't turn the radio off, or find another station. The silly tune would be over in a couple of minutes. Hearing it, she could almost feel Steve's arm about her, the touch of his chin against her hair. Almost, but not quite. And she would never be dancing with Steve again. Marcy felt quite sure of that.

Oh, they had quarreled before. But not like last night. There had been such an air of finality about the way he had driven off. Marcy had been able to twist the old Steve around her finger. But this new one, this more mature Steve—well, he was very different. He wouldn't take what the old Steve had taken at Marcy's hands. He was quite through with her.

And I'm through with him! Marcy thought. Him and his Thea. He can just go back to college and date her all the time. I don't care!

But she knew she was only kidding herself. She didn't really mean it.

At last the tune that hurt so was over. Marcy took up another spoonful of cereal and sat staring at it.

"So there you are." Ken's voice behind her made Marcy jump and slosh milk onto the table. "Why are you being so exclusive and eating all by yourself?"

Marcy forced a cheerful smile as she mopped up the milk with a napkin. "You were sleeping so peacefully, I couldn't bear to disturb you."

"Mighty considerate all of a sudden, aren't you?" Ken

was wearing his corduroy robe over gaudy red-and-yellow printed pajamas. His bare feet were thrust into fleece-lined moccasins. He yawned and stretched, then sat down opposite Marcy and helped himself to fruit juice. Putting bread into the toaster, he asked, "What happened to you and Steve last night?"

From his manner, Marcy judged that he hadn't seen Steve, that he didn't know they'd quarreled. Of course, he'd hear about it eventually, but she couldn't face telling him the details right now. "Oh, we drove around," she evaded.

"So did we," Ken grinned, "but we stopped in at the Sweet Shop later. Most of the gang were there, all but you two."

"Did you miss us?" Marcy kept her tone light and casual.

"Sure," Ken said. "It was sort of a reunion."

Marcy asked, "How did Rosemary seem after all your dates with college girls, pretty young and naive?"

Ken shook his head. "She's okay. Only—" he stared at Marcy thoughtfully for a moment, "she was telling me about this new club of yours, this 'widows' deal."

Marcy smiled. "We have lots of fun."

Ken frowned. "I think you're nuts, every last one of you," he said, buttering the toast that had just popped up.

"It's really none of your business," Marcy flared, "so long as we enjoy it!"

"Kind of touchy, aren't you?" Ken's tone was mild. "I'm only trying to give you some brotherly advice, all for free."

"Who wants advice?" Marcy demanded. "Especially from someone who doesn't know a thing about it? You're off at college, where everything's new and different and things are happening all the time. But we're stuck here in Westfield, and it's pretty dull around school. Being a senior isn't much fun when all the fellows we used to date are away at college."

Ken asked, still in that mild, easygoing tone that so annoyed Marcy, "There are some senior boys, aren't there? You don't want to give up just because Steve's away and the competition may be a bit rough."

Marcy glared at him. "You men make me sick! It's simple enough for you. All you have to do is ask a girl, any girl, for a date. But a girl has to wait till she's asked!"

"Just a minute," Ken said firmly. "A girl has to give a guy the idea he wouldn't be wasting his time. He isn't going to go out hunting for her with a lantern, like Diogenes looking for an honest man. If you want a guy to ask you for a date, you have to be the kind of girl he'd have some fun spending his hardearned money on. And you certainly don't give that impression with all this silly business of calling yourselves 'widows' and moping around together."

"We don't mope!" Marcy informed him. "There just aren't any boys at school I'm interested in."

Ken hooted derisively. "Don't hand me that. If I remember correctly, you didn't think you were interested in Steve till you got to know him pretty well. Most fellows improve on acquaintance, you know."

"That's different," Marcy said, "altogether different. I was much younger when I began getting interested in

Steve. I hadn't had any dates before. I couldn't make comparisons."

Ken grinned. "You mean if you'd had someone to compare Steve with, he wouldn't have made the grade, either? You are getting hard to suit!"

"I mean—" Marcy began and stopped. What she had meant was that, having known Steve, she hadn't been able to find any boys around who measured up to him. But she didn't feel that way any longer. She was mad at Steve, the double-crosser! She was through with him. But she didn't want to go into all that with Ken. Not yet. Not while her feelings were still so raw with the hurt of it that she might start crying again. "Oh," she demanded, jumping up, "why should I explain all my feelings to you? Just because you're home for a few days, you needn't start trying to boss me around. Being in college doesn't make you such a big shot—nor Steve Judson, either!"

Ken just sat there, grinning at her, which made Marcy angrier than ever. Glaring, she turned on her heel and stalked from the room.

"Where you going?" Ken called after her.

"Over to Liz's," Marcy informed him coldly.

Ken offered, "If you're around this afternoon, I'll take you up for a plane ride. I'm going out to the airport and rent one for half an hour. I haven't piloted a plane more than a couple of times since last summer and I have to keep my hand in."

"How will you get there?" Marcy asked. "Dad's got the car. He drives every day now and drops Mom off at the hospital."

During the moment's silence while Ken considered this, Marcy felt a surge of eagerness rise in her. If they could get to the airport, it would be fun to go up with Ken again. He had worked there last summer, taking most of his pay in flying lessons, and had got his pilot's license shortly before he left for college. She had only flown with him a few times, but she loved it.

Finally Ken said, "I'll see if I can't borrow a car. Bix Meyers', maybe, or Steve's folks' bus."

"I'll go if you can get one," Marcy told him. "See you later."

She thought she'd feel a little better after she had told Liz all about her scrap with Steve. But Liz didn't prove very sympathetic. "Honestly," she scolded Marcy, "you have a perfectly diabolical knack of fighting with a guy at the wrong time! When he's only home for a few days—and you've been waiting all fall for him to get home—" Liz broke off with a sigh.

"But don't you think I was justified?" Marcy demanded.

"Gee, I don't know," Liz said. "It seems to me he only did what you'd both agreed to."

"Oh, let's not hash it over any more!" Marcy exclaimed. "We're all washed up, so there's no use discussing it."

"Okay," Liz said, "if that's how you feel."

After a moment's brooding silence, Marcy asked, "What did you do last night?"

A faint smile curved Liz's lips. "I had a terrific time," she admitted. And she went on to tell Marcy all about it. "Hank and I had a date and after the show we stopped in at the Sweet Shop. And there was practically all our old gang from last year and guess what!"

"I don't know," Marcy shook her head, "unless Bill Weaver got home after all."

"From Texas?" Liz demanded. "Don't be silly! No, but Buzz Merrill was there. And he'd brought his roommate from Purdue home with him for the holidays." It seemed that this young man, whose name was Tom Harris, was as handsome and attractive as any movie star. And he had shown signs of marked interest in Liz, so much so that Hank had been pea-green with jealousy. "Of course," Liz explained happily, "I didn't really neglect Hank for Tom, because Hank's the one who'll be around long after Tom's gone. But it was such fun to have the two of them sort of hovering at my elbows and glaring at each other. And I'm keeping my fingers crossed that maybe Tom will call up today and—" Liz chattered on and Marcy listened, putting in a word often enough to convince her friend that she was really being attentive. But her thoughts were glumly preoccupied with her own problems. And her face must have shown the depths of her misery, because finally Liz broke off to say contritely, "Gee, Marce, I'm sorry. I didn't mean to rub it in. Maybe," she added, obviously trying to cheer Marcy, "Steve will drop over to see you today and you can patch things up. I hope so."

Marcy shook her head. "Steve and I are through."

"You always feel that way," Liz reminded her, "when you've had a fight." She asked then, "If he called up or came over, you'd see him, wouldn't you?"

Marcy explained, "If he comes over this afternoon, which he certainly isn't likely to, I won't be there."

"You mean you've got a date," Liz asked interestedly, "with someone else?"

Marcy laughed, a hollow, not very mirthful sound. "If he can borrow a car to get us out to the airport," she told her friend, "I'm going flying with my brother."

"Oh," Liz said.

❧ ELEVEN ❧

Ken Talks Turkey

KEN WASN'T AROUND WHEN MARCY GOT home from Liz's house. She spent the rest of the morning dutifully making beds and washing dishes, straightening up generally. Everything was spic-and-span by one o'clock and Marcy was getting hungry. She wandered out to the kitchen to make herself some lunch, tired of waiting for Ken. She didn't even know where he had gone, although she supposed he was out trying to borrow a car.

No sooner had she sat down with a Dagwood-type double-decker, made up of left-over turkey and stuffing and cranberry sauce, than she heard a sound of car wheels on the drive. Marcy looked out the window and there was Ken, just climbing out of Bix Meyers' car.

"I see you got one," she greeted him as he came in the back door.

"I twisted Bix's arm," Ken said cheerfully. "I can only have it an hour or so, but that's long enough. You ready?"

"Don't you want something to eat?" Marcy waved her sandwich at him enticingly.

"Nah," Ken said. "Haven't got time now. Bring your grub along and eat on the way. I'm dying for the feel of some wide open air under me."

Marcy gulped down her milk and had Ken hold her sandwich while she shrugged into a warm coat and caught up her woolen scarf and mittens. It would be cold flying, she suspected.

When Ken handed her sandwich back, it had shrunk considerably.

"Fine thing!" Marcy accused him, "You ate half my lunch!"

Her brother grinned at her as they got into Bix's old car. "I just can't resist those crazy concoctions of yours!"

The airport was only a few miles out of town. As they drove along, Marcy eyed the bright blue cloudless sky and felt joyous anticipation rise in her.

She asked Ken, "I'll bet you miss flying, don't you?"

Her brother nodded. "Sure do. I've rented a plane a couple of times down at school, but I can't afford to fly very often." He grinned, "I've been saving up for to-day."

Marcy smiled back at him. "I appreciate your taking me with you. After all, I'm just your sister."

Ken said wryly, "The only time I ever took Rosemary up, she hung onto me for dear life, scared to death."

"How nice for you," Marcy laughed.

But Ken shook his head. "Not when I had to pilot the plane. If we'd gone high enough, I could have set the controls and given her my full attention. But she had a fit if I did much more than clear the treetops.

That's the trouble with people who aren't used to flying. They feel safer the lower they are, when actually the higher you fly, the less danger there is. But try to persuade Rosemary of that!"

The owner of the little airport, Hank Carlson, greeted Ken with a friendly grin and handshake. "Thought you'd be coming out for a spin if you got home over the holidays." He told Marcy, "This big brother of yours is a pretty fair pilot, if I do say it as shouldn't, seeing as how I taught him."

"Just don't take all the credit," Ken kidded him. "Look at the great material you had to work with."

Marcy waited in the main hangar where it was warm, while Ken helped wheel a little red plane out onto the runway. He and Hank attended to gassing it and preparing it for flight. The motor was roaring, as if impatient to be off, when Marcy slid in beside Ken on the scuffed leather seat. She waved at Hank and leaned just a bit closer to her brother's solid shoulder.

"Boy, this feels good," Ken told her, his hands sure on the controls, his eyes squinting slightly in concentration. He had to shout to make her hear above the motor's noise.

Marcy nodded, feeling a sense of exhilaration swell in her as the plane sped along the runway, its rate of speed increasing until, almost without her realizing it, they became airborne. Now they moved much more smoothly, mounting gradually, circling the field where the sprawling hangar, in which she had so recently stood, grew ever smaller. Marcy leaned back against the leather cushions, away from the heartening feel of Ken's shoulder, her momentary nervousness gone. The roar of the motor made conversation practically impossible. But neither of them felt inclined to talk. Ken gestured now and then, pointing out some landmark, and Marcy looked down, recognizing it with a smile and nod. There was Westfield High, seeming no more than doll-house size. Beyond it the football field was spread out like a drab, greenish brown handkerchief.

"Our house," Ken said, indicating it among the black lace of leafless trees far below.

Marcy lip-read his words and looked down, locating the white blur of the tiny building at last. It didn't even look familiar from this bird's-eye view. All the houses seemed like nothing more impressive than a child's building project scattered across some playroom floor.

She lifted her glance and let it rest on the blue of the sky beyond the plane's windows. A sense of detachment settled over her, a feeling of complete serenity and peace. Some lines of poetry drifted through her mind, something she had read and not quite forgotten.

Oh, I have slipped the surly bonds of earth
And danced the skies on laughter-silvered wings—

And there was more to it. Something about "—put out my hand and touch the face of God."

Flying, Marcy thought, made you feel like that. Free and happy and, at the same time, deeply reverent. It made you rather starkly aware, too, of your own unimportance in the overall scheme of things. And you felt a little ashamed of your smallness, and anxious to grow and to achieve something worthwhile. You knew, too, a hope that someday you would become a wiser and more mature person, worthy of at least a little bit of the time and trouble God had taken with the human race.

Marcy wondered whether Ken was experiencing any of these sensations that flowed through her. But the motor was far too noisy for her to ask. And later, after they had landed, the urge to make such profound queries had faded away. Marcy realized painfully that her fingers and toes were almost frozen. And so they lingered, warming up in Hank Carlson's stuffy little office, talking casually with him while the radio blared a raucous accompaniment.

"That was just what I needed," Ken said enthusiastically as he and Marcy got into Bix's car once more. "You enjoy it, too?"

Marcy nodded. "I loved it, I always do." She still felt chilled, though, and said as much.

"Me, too," Ken admitted. "Tell you what. Let's stop at the diner down the road for a hamburger and something hot to drink. That should fix us up."

"Swell," Marcy agreed.

The roadside restaurant was deserted at this hour. Having brought their order, the waitress ambled back into the kitchen and they had the place entirely to themselves.

Eating her hamburger, sipping her hot chocolate, Marcy gradually thawed out. Both she and Ken devoted all their attention to food for a few minutes.

Then Ken said, his blue glance direct on her face, "I want to talk to you."

"More brotherly advice, all for free?" Marcy asked drily.

"I think you need it," Ken told her. "What's the idea,

holding out on me that you and Steve had a big scrap last night?"

"Is there a law that says I have to tell you everything?" Marcy demanded. "Apparently you heard all the details from Steve, anyway, so what does it matter?"

"Steve was feeling mighty low when I stopped by to try to borrow their car," Ken informed her. "His mother had it out somewhere, but poor old Steve was glad to get a chance to unburden himself to somebody. You must have given him a rough deal last night."

"I gave *him* a rough deal!" Marcy glared at her brother. "All you heard was his side of it!"

Ken took a bite of his hamburger, chewed it deliberately, and swallowed. "Let's hear your side," he suggested.

"I prefer not to discuss it." Unconsciously Marcy lifted her chin. "Steve Judson is not important enough for me to waste time on. He can just go back to college and date his Thea Cunningham as often as he likes. I don't care! It was simply the idea of his sneaking behind my back that made me so mad."

"Jealous," Ken murmured, wagging his head sadly.

"I'm not!" Marcy denied.

"Please," Ken's tone was coaxing. "It's just that an interested bystander, who's sympathetic, but not actually involved, often sees a situation like this so much more clearly than the participants. As I get the picture, you're burned up at Steve for doing something you both agreed was a good idea."

"But—" Marcy began. And stopped. Because what Ken said was true enough. She contented herself with merely sipping her hot chocolate in aloof silence.

"You see?" Ken said. "You can't deny that's how it is. You're sore about a girl he dated a few times at college. But last summer you thought he was all wrong when he felt the same way about that guy you met out in Colorado. So if Steve was wrong then, you're wrong now. Or, if he was right last summer, you had no cause to get mad at him then. See? It comes out even."

There must be some sound argument against her brother's logic, but Marcy couldn't think of it. She continued to stare down stubbornly into her cup, not saying anything.

"Look, kid," Ken's tone was gentle. "Steve still likes you best. He's sunk about last night. He's looked forward to Thanksgiving—"

"I've looked forward to it, too!" Marcy broke in, her voice low and a little chokey. "I've been counting the days. It hasn't been any fun since Steve left—not any fun at all! I haven't had a single date, while he—" she couldn't go on.

"That," Ken told her earnestly, "was where you made your mistake. You shouldn't have just sat home mooning over him, building him up in your mind into some sort of super-man type he couldn't possibly live up to. It's not fair to him and it's not fair to yourself, either."

The sympathy in her brother's tone broke down the last of Marcy's defenses. And suddenly, she was telling him exactly how things had been, pouring out the whole muddled, unhappy story of the past few months, so long shut up within her.

When she had finished, Ken said quietly, "You sure got off on the wrong foot this year, didn't you?"

Marcy couldn't deny it. "Everything's been such a

mess," she said flatly. "At school, at home—everywhere! Nothing worked out the way I wanted it."

Ken said, after a moment's thoughtful silence, "I think part of your trouble is, you've kind of pulled back into your shell. You figure you're licked before you start, so you won't make an effort. And to justify your attitude, you tell yourself that none of the fellows at school interest you. So, maybe they aren't terrific, but they're better than nothing."

A faint smile twitched at Marcy's lips. "Now you sound like Liz." Still, she didn't shut her mind entirely to the possibility that there might be something in what Ken said. He had given her some darned good advice in the past. At least, she'd hear him out.

He leaned a little nearer, his elbows on the narrow table between them, his eyes intent. "Then Liz is on the right track," he said. "You'd better listen to her."

"But I told you—" Marcy began.

Ken wouldn't let her finish. "I've got a terrific idea!" he exclaimed.

"Oh, no!" Marcy said faintly. She had had some experience in the past with Ken's bright ideas.

"Will you promise to do it?" he asked.

"Not," Marcy said positively, "till I hear what it is." But she felt a little lift of excitement just the same.

"Do it as a favor for me," Ken coaxed, "just so I can prove a pet theory of mine is correct. Pick a guy at school," he went on, "any guy. For instance, the one who happens to sit next to you in English. Then concentrate on him. Be agreeable and friendly. Get better acquainted. Learn what he's like, what makes him tick. If he's the quiet type, meet him a little more than halfway. I don't mean chase him. Just use your own good sense. But let him see that you're aware he's around, that you're willing to be friends. And you know what I'll bet?"

Marcy shook her head, intrigued in spite of herself. She had forgotten how persuasive Ken could be when he tried.

"I'll bet," her brother told her, "that you'll find you like him, at least fairly well. And I'll also bet he'll ask you for a date. Is it a deal?"

Marcy scoffed, "You're absolutely crazy, you and your theories!"

"Crazy or not," Ken argued, "I'll bet it will work. Only you probably haven't got enough spizzerinctum to try it."

Marcy had to laugh. "Now you're using psychology on me," she accused. But she felt herself weakening. She never could hold out against Ken. Besides, what harm could his absurd experiment do? It wouldn't work, of course, but it might be sort of interesting to try out.

"Okay," she told him finally, "it's a deal."

"Good," Ken said. He stuck out his hand and Marcy put hers into it, binding the bargain, just as they used to do when they were children. "And be sure to write and keep me informed how it's going," he told her.

"Or how it isn't going." Marcy nodded ruefully.

Still, the hard clasp of his hand on hers seemed to lift just a little the weight of glum misery that had pressed down on Marcy all day. Maybe, she thought, things weren't quite so bleak as they had seemed. Maybe.

❧ TWELVE ❧

Good–bye Again

MARCY AND KEN LEFT BIX'S CAR AT HIS house and walked the short distance home. Ken asked, "Got any plans for tonight?"

Marcy shook her head. "The Widows" weren't meeting this particular Friday. She had been as strongly in favor of skipping their meeting as the others. Now, with Steve out of the picture, she was completely at loose ends.

Ken said, "You know what you'd do if you weren't chicken, don't you?" Then, at Marcy's questioning look, he went on, "you'd call Steve up and apologize. He rates it and you know he does. You're the one who's in the wrong."

"Well, I won't call him," Marcy said flatly.

A nagging suspicion that Ken might be right gnawed at her. But a girl had her pride.

"That's what I thought," Ken said disgustedly. "Trust a woman to make a guy take the initiative every time!"

They walked the rest of the way home in silence. As they went up the front steps, Ken began whistling.

"What's that song?" Marcy asked in the hallway. "I like it."

"Oh, that?" Ken said. "Just our fraternity song. Beta Zeta, Brothers All."

The tune kept running through Marcy's head even after Ken had stopped whistling. Very catchy, it was, with a brisk swing to it. Ken prowled around the house restlessly, read for a while, played some old jazz records. Marcy ironed a couple of slips and a blouse she had washed out by hand. The job wasn't nearly so boring with Ken around to talk to occasionally. Just knowing he was in the house helped.

He came out to the kitchen as Marcy was putting the ironing board away. "Why don't you make something exotic for dinner," he suggested. "Like strawberry torte."

Marcy smiled. That was Ken's favorite dessert. "I guess I could make one for you when you were nice enough to take me flying."

"Attagirl," he laid an affectionate arm across her shoulder. "I've been drooling for it for months."

He ambled off as Marcy got out mixing bowl and electric beater and began assembling ingredients. Above the whirr of the mixer, she heard him talking on the phone, but his words were unintelligible. Probably making plans with Rosemary for the evening, Marcy thought wistfully. A tide of loneliness for Steve, of regret for last night, rose in her. Pride seemed rather an inadequate shield against the emptiness their quarrel had left in her heart.

Just as she finished putting the torte in the oven,

Marcy heard the doorbell chime. "Ken?" she called apprehensively, brushing at the flour on her hands and apron.

But Ken didn't answer. And now Marcy became aware of the sound of running water from the bathroom. Obviously, Ken was taking a shower. A faint frown of annoyance between her eyes, Marcy went to answer the repeated summons.

Her heart lurched as she opened the door and saw Steve standing there. For a moment she couldn't say a thing.

Steve, too, seemed to be having some difficulty finding words. Finally he managed, "Ken around?"

Marcy nodded. "He's in the shower," she explained. And then, not too enthusiastically, added, "Won't you come in?"

Steve came. He took off his jacket and dropped it on a chair. He looked as ill at ease and unhappy as Marcy felt. The sound of running water continued unabated from upstairs.

"Sit down if you like," Marcy motioned vaguely toward the couch. "He should be through soon."

"Thanks," Steve said.

They might have been two strangers, Marcy thought desolately. Why in the world has Steve come? He could just as well have phoned Ken, thus avoiding this awkward unnecessary encounter. Phoned? A sudden light began to break over her.

She asked Steve, "Did Ken call you up?"

Steve nodded. "Yeah, just a little while ago. Said he had something important to tell me, something he couldn't go into on the phone."

Marcy felt righteous anger rise in her at her brother and his devious scheming. So that was it! This was all an elaborate plot to bring Steve and her together. Ken had phoned, then hid in the bathroom, leaving her to let Steve in. Ken had figured that when they saw each other, she'd weaken and say she was sorry—or that Steve would.

"Say!" Steve grinned faintly. "You don't suppose—?"

Marcy couldn't seem to stop her own lips from curving into an answering smile. "I'm afraid so. You know Ken and his string-pulling. We—" her voice sort of wobbled, "we'll just have to show him his plot won't work."

"Yeah," Steve said, his grin fading slowly. "Yeah, I guess so."

"I'll go up and hammer on the bathroom door till he—"

"Let me go," Steve broke in. "I can pound harder."

"Okay."

But he didn't go. He just stood there, looking at her. And Marcy stood looking at him. She couldn't seem to pull her eyes away.

Finally Steve said, his voice reproachful, "You had a lot of nerve, treating me the way you did last night."

Marcy opened her mouth to argue. But the conviction that Steve was right choked off the words. Instead, she surprised herself by saying in a small, rather quavery voice, "I think so, too. And—" this was much harder to say, but Marcy managed it, "and I'm sorry."

"You are?" Steve's stare was blank for a moment. Then a light broke across his face. He reached out to grab Marcy's arms and pull her close. "Gee," he said then, his voice husky, "so am I."

It must have been all of fifteen minutes later that Ken came quietly down the stairs and stuck his head around the edge of the door. Marcy and Steve were sitting quite close together on the couch, Steve's arm around her and his dark sport shirt smudged with flour.

"It's about time," Ken said plaintively. "I was beginning to shrivel in that tub." Suddenly he frowned. "How about the torte? No use burning it on the altar of young love."

"Oh, my gosh!" Marcy jumped up. "The torte!"

She flew for the kitchen with the two boys close behind. But the torte wasn't ruined. It had baked just right, to a delicate golden tan. As she set it carefully on the cooling rack, Marcy laughed at her brother, "You really deserved to have it burn, you and your finagling with my affairs."

"Your affairs?" Ken demanded. "I was merely helping a fraternity brother out of a bad spot."

"I'm grateful, boy," Steve said and grinned at him.

Marcy was grateful, too, even though she wouldn't give Ken the satisfaction of hearing her come right out and admit it. But their eyes met in a look of understanding . . .

The rest of that week end passed in an enchanted dream. Marcy and Steve spent most of their time together. They went bowling with the old crowd, doubledated with Ken and Rosemary for dinner and a stage show in Clay City. They had sodas at the Sweet Shop, went for drives, listened to records and talked endlessly. It was like old times, warm and wonderful. It was the way Marcy had imagined the Thanksgiving holiday would be. The stormy interval at the beginning only made the rest of the time seem smoother and more fun. But, like all good things, it had to end.

During their last date, Steve told Marcy, "Our fraternity gives a big dance on the eighteenth of December. The Firehouse Follies, it's called, and I want you to come down for it. Will you?"

Marcy felt her heart lift with heady excitement at the idea. "I'd love to," she told Steve. And then, her voice earnest, "But I don't want you to feel you have to ask me, just because I was so unreasonable about—Thea and everything. If you'd rather go with her—"

"If I would," Steve informed her, "I'd have asked her instead of you. It's all settled then."

"All settled," Marcy agreed.

She had heard a little about the Firehouse Follies and its origin from Ken. Now Steve proceeded to enlighten her even more fully. It seemed that some years earlier the fire department of a town near the college had decided to invest in new equipment. Their old engine, still basically sound, but much the worse for wear, had been put up for sale at public auction. The bidding, however, proved slow and the Beta Zetas had been able to buy the old engine for a nominal sum and drive it gleefully back to the fraternity house. Since then it had been refurbished with a new coat of scarlet paint and its metal work had been polished to a fine glow. A new motor had been installed and the fire engine, lovingly christened Beezee in an elaborate ceremony, was now used as a general utility car, in place of the small truck or station wagon owned by the other fraternities.

Naturally, the brothers were not slow to realize Beezee's many other possibilities. The engine was used to transport the boys' dance dates from their residence halls or sorority houses. It also served as the motivating theme of their biggest dance of the year.

"But I don't want to tell you all about it," Steve stopped himself. "It'll be more fun if you're surprised."

Marcy thought so, too, and didn't press him for further details. She couldn't smother a small rapturous sigh at the thought of being a part of it all . . .

On Sunday, when Ken's out-of-town fraternity brother stopped by to pick him up for the trip back to college, Steve was already in the car. But Marcy had no chance for even one really personal word with him. There was the flurry of introductions, the rush and scramble of stowing Ken's bag in the already crowded back seat, then the good-byes.

"Remember," Ken told her pointedly, "about our big deal. I'll be expecting to hear from you on it pronto."

Marcy smiled dubiously. Her reconciliation with Steve and all the wonderful fun that had followed it had driven the thought of Ken's absurd theory out of her mind. Now she said, her tone noncommittal, "Well, we'll see."

"See, my foot!" Ken said firmly. "We shook hands on it, remember?"

Marcy only had time to nod, to feel her fingers squeezed hard in Steve's for a moment, to hear his voice saying, "See you down at school in a few weeks."

Then she was standing on the curb with Mom and Dad, waving at the departing car, feeling a little ache of loss catch at her throat.

"Well," Dad said, putting his arm across Mom's

shoulders as they walked back toward the house, "that's that."

Mom nodded. "It was wonderful to have him home," she said softly. "But now we'll miss him worse than ever."

Mom was speaking of Ken. Marcy was thinking of Steve and Ken. Still, she felt her mother's words covered the situation pretty well.

❧ THIRTEEN ❧

Once Upon a Week End

MARCY DECIDED NOT TO TELL EVEN LIZ about the screwy plan Ken had talked her into. She was sure it wouldn't work, so why make a big thing of it? Besides, Liz was thrilled enough over Marcy's invitation to the Firehouse Follies. They discussed that endlessly and with no abatement of enjoyment.

"You just don't realize how lucky you are," Liz said wistfully. "A real college week end. The whole thing sounds so terrific! If only that louse Bill hadn't gone all the way to Texas to school!"

"Maybe he'll come home this summer in boots and a ten-gallon hat," Marcy offered.

"A lot of good that'll do me," Liz griped.

"Maybe Buzz Merrill's friend—what was his name?— will ask you to Purdue for a dance," Marcy tried to cheer her up.

But Liz shook her blond head sadly. "Tom was nice, but I'm sure I didn't make that much of an impression on him in one week end, especially with Hank glowering at him all the time." She shrugged philosophically, "Oh, well, I've still got Hank. And you know what? The guy grows on you. He's lots of fun and really more intelligent than Bill."

Marcy nodded. Her attitude toward Hank seemed to have mellowed some. She told Liz, "Ken was saying that almost any boy seems more interesting, the better you get to know him." She smiled, remembering her recent talks with Ken. "He took a very dim view of 'The Widows,' just as you do."

"Well, good," Liz said. "I hope he talked some sense into you."

"I guess he talked some into Rosemary, too," Marcy admitted. "She's not so keen on the club any more, either. And Donna Hepple's started dating that new boy who just moved here from Cleveland. So, we've decided to disband. The club didn't turn out to be as much fun as we thought it would."

Liz said, "Now if you'll only start dating somebody."

Marcy smiled at her. "I guess I'll look over the material at hand, at least . . ."

It would have been easy that next week to get discouraged and begin living in the future again, dreaming about the absent Steve and looking forward to the fraternity dance, but Marcy resisted the temptation. "Pick a guy," Ken had said, "any guy. Maybe the one who sits next to you in English." To follow this suggestion literally would have been quite useless. Marcy was surrounded on three sides in her English class by girls. And to her left sat Bruce Douglas, with his close-cut blond hair and easy smile, his habit of friendliness to everyone that had made him one of the most popular—and pursued—members of the senior class. Bruce was president of the Student Council, he had the lead cinched in the senior play, he had won his letter at basketball and was good at several other sports as well. Marcy would only be wasting her time to pick Bruce as a candidate in Ken's experiment. Bruce always said, "Hi," to her in his pleasant manner. But Marcy knew that actually he wasn't aware of her at all.

She looked around speculatively in some of her other classes. Her best bet seemed to be in Study Hall. Carl Johnson sat behind her there and Rick Whitney to her right. Carl had curly dark hair and a quick grin. Rick was tall and thin and quiet, but nice enough looking. Marcy said an inaudible eenie-meenie and decided to try Carl. She broke the ice by asking him about an assignment, then managed so that they walked out of Study Hall side by side. Scarcely had they reached the corridor, though, still in animated conversation, when they were joined by Eileen Clark. And Eileen's proprietary manner and the pointed way she took Carl over made clear to the discomfited Marcy that Carl had a large "Hands Off" sign hung on him, at least in the other girl's estimation. Marcy hoped the hot embarrassed color that rushed to her face wasn't too obvious.

Later, when she asked Liz about Eileen and Carl, her friend told her, "Oh, sure, they're going steady. Why do you ask?"

"Just wondering," Marcy evaded. "Sort of looking over the field, you know." She asked then, because Liz seemed better informed than she on such matters, "How about Rick Whitney? Anyone got dibs on him?"

Liz considered thoughtfully. "I don't think so. But he's so quiet. You haven't really got a yen for him, have you?"

Marcy smiled, shaking her head. "I was just thinking about him as a possibility. Maybe he's sort of shy."

"Maybe," Liz agreed. "But he sure wouldn't be an easy person to get to know."

Even so, Marcy thought, she might have a go at him tomorrow. She was going to have to do something. Ken had been needling her ever since he went back to college. Almost every day when Marcy got home, there'd be a postcard from Ken awaiting her. One had said simply, "Well, have you tried it? I'm dying for a full report." Another admonished, "Quit stalling! Remember you promised." There had been others in similar vein. Marcy knew she'd have no peace from Ken till she did something definite about his silly theory and wrote him the result. Maybe Rick would be as likely a starting point as she could find.

But that evening when Marcy was finishing the book report which was her English assignment, something happened that drove all thought of Rick, or even of Steve, out of her mind, at least for the time being.

The phone rang and Marcy answered it. The male voice at the other end of the wire was unfamiliar and yet, in some tantalizing way, she was sure she'd heard it before.

"Marcy?" the voice asked. Then, at her affirmative, it went on, a little undernote of laughter warming the words, "I reckon you'd never guess who this is."

It was the "reckon" that gave Marcy a clue. She felt her heart begin to hammer, tried to tell herself it was impossible even as her lips formed the name. "Noel?"

"How'd you guess?" he asked aggrievedly. "I was plannin' to string you along and keep you guessin'. How are you, Marcy?"

"Well, fine—" she felt choked and breathless. "But where are you? How on earth—?"

His chuckle came along the wire, slow and deep, just as she remembered it. "Chicago," he told her. "My dad's here, too. We brought some cutting horses to show at the Live Stock Exhibition here at the Stock Yards."

As Marcy listened to his voice, telling her all about it, she felt again the stir of excitement he had aroused in her last summer. Noel, she thought, still a little incredulous. Noel Cramer only some thirty miles away, talking with her on the phone.

She had thought she'd never see him or hear from him again. He had seemed like a part of another life, sealed away from the present. Now here he was, real and actual again, and as exciting as ever. Marcy could scarcely breathe with the sheer wonder of it.

She asked him how his brother, Tack, was and the rest of his family. She inquired about the friends she had made last summer, Cindy Bayliss, and the others. Now and then she heard Noel deposit another coin and realized he must be calling on a pay phone.

"This is costing you lots of money," Marcy reminded.

But Noel told her, "It's worth it." He went on then to get to the cause of his call, above and beyond a mere urge to talk with her. Would it be possible, he wanted to know, for her to take a train in to the city on Saturday and meet him for dinner and the evening? They could see the final night of the Stock Show and he could drive her home in the car his father had rented for the duration of their stay.

"It sounds wonderful," Marcy told him. "Maybe you could stay out here overnight then. My parents would love to meet you." She knew she didn't have to ask them. Mom's and Dad's beaming enthusiastic faces, their nods of agreement, were clearly visible to her in the living-room doorway.

"Well," Noel drawled in a pleased tone, "if you're sure it'd be okay with them. I'd like to meet them, too. But I'll have to leave pretty early Sunday. Dad and I are catching the train for Colorado Springs around noon sometime."

When all the details had been settled and Marcy had said good-bye and hung up, she stood for a moment, leaning against the wall, a happy smile curving her mouth, her eyes shining. Seeing her so, her parents waited until she came out of her dreaming daze before they began asking the interested questions that crowded to their lips. But it was several minutes before Marcy came down to earth sufficiently to begin telling them all about it . . .

The next day, Friday, dragged past so slowly Marcy kept checking her watch to be sure it hadn't stopped.

"If only," Liz said dolefully when Marcy told her what had happened, "they'd brought Tack along, too. Then we could have double-dated, just like last summer."

But she snapped out of her regretful mood almost at once and was happy in Marcy's pleasure. They discussed what Marcy should wear. They reminisced endlessly over all the fun they'd had at Liz's uncle's ranch.

"Do you suppose," Liz wondered aloud, "it's going to seem sort of strange to be with Noël, when you haven't seen each other for months and after he asked you to marry him and all?"

"I'll simply act," Marcy told her, "as though he hadn't asked me. And he didn't seem stiff or strange a bit on the telephone. We were more easy with each other last night when we talked than I was with Steve—" She broke off to tell Liz, her eyes widening in astonishment, "Why, do you know I haven't even thought about Steve for a whole day!"

Liz grinned. "Seems to me Noël put him out of your mind for quite a while last summer, too."

"I wonder," Marcy murmured, her tone troubled, "if I'm really fickle. I'm awfully fond of both of them."

"That's not being fickle," Liz argued. "You're just too young to be sure who you like best. It might turn out to be Steve, or Noël, or more likely someone you haven't even met yet."

Marcy nodded absently, busy with her own thoughts . . .

From the moment when Noël met her in the big echoing train shed Saturday evening, Marcy felt the inexplicable magic of last summer begin to envelop her once more. It wasn't entirely his tall, rangy good looks, or the droll, easygoing charm of his manner. But a glow of warmth and happiness seemed to flare up in her in his presence. She felt so at ease with him, whether they were talking or silent, laughing or serious.

All during the evening it was like that. They had wonderful steaks at a small table in the Stock Yards

Inn. But for all Marcy knew they could have been eating hamburgers. Noel's hazel eyes looking deep into hers, the low sound of his laugh, the accidental touch of his big hand as he helped her with her coat—these were the important things that Marcy would remember.

"How's my rival?" Noel asked not too seriously, "That fella named Steve you told me about last summer—is he still around?"

Marcy explained about Steve being away at college. "I saw him Thanksgiving," she finished, "and we write."

Noel grinned. "I'm no hand at letter writing myself. Get all bogged down in them and—" he shrugged, "they never say what I mean, so I end up firing them into the wastebasket."

Marcy wondered whether he might have tried to write her some letters. Aside from one rather stilted note soon after her return from Colorado, she'd had no word from him until now. But she didn't voice the question. There seemed no point in doing so. It was enough that Noel had called her when he had the chance, when it was possible for them to be together.

Marcy hadn't attended a stock show since she was a child. She had forgotten how much fun it was to watch the various events. First came the parade of prize winning horses and cattle, then the exhibition of sheep dogs, herding their charges into the pens provided. Marcy thrilled to the rhythmic precision of the six-horse teams, drawing the big red-and-gold wagons around the tanbark arena. There were several horse stakes involving the winners of earlier events, since this was the final night of the show. The nervous, patrician trotters pulled their little two-wheeled carts, the five-gaited horses went through their impressive paces, the big powerful hunters jumped their barricades. There were also the finals of the cutting-horse exhibitions. These latter revealed a thrilling display of skill and agility on the part of both horse and rider in cutting a single steer out of a herd bent and determined to stay together.

Noel, Marcy learned, had ridden in some of the cutting-horse exhibitions during earlier days of the show. "But I got eliminated," he told her with his slow grin. "Otherwise I'd be out there ridin' and you'd have to watch these finals by yourself."

"I don't see how it happened," Marcy said loyally. She remembered his riding in the rodeo last summer at the Kendall ranch and how wonderful he had been. "You ride so well."

Noel shook his head. "I'm just merely mediocre," he said, but his eyes were warm with appreciation. "I found that out for sure in this kind of competition—but it was fun."

Afterward, there was the long drive out from the city through the chill night, with stars pale and faraway overhead. A dreamy contentment wrapped Marcy about as they left the lights of the city behind and swept out along the broad highway through the scattered suburban towns. They talked or were silent and it didn't matter which, since even the quiet moments that fell upon them were companionable.

Once Marcy murmured regretfully, "I wish you didn't live so far away. It's been so nice seeing you again." Yet even as she spoke the words, she realized that Noel wasn't really quite at home in his neat gray suit and striped necktie. His broad shoulders and lean height cried out for the gay western shirt and Levi's he usually wore. And his bare head needed the broad-brimmed Stetson, which had seemed so much a part of him in Colorado.

Noel said drily, "I'd be like a fish out of water around here. Big cities make me feel all penned in and unhappy. All those skyscrapers shuttin' out the sky, and the crowds of people hurryin' along the streets and not even lookin' up—" He shook his head ruefully.

Marcy explained to him that Westfield was just a little town, not like the city a bit. "You won't mind it there so much."

Noel chuckled. "Maybe not." He asked then, "You don't suppose I can prevail on your folks to move out to Colorado?"

He was joking of course. But the remark seemed to indicate that he'd missed her, that he'd like to see her more often. Marcy sighed a small blissful sigh and wished this wonderful night never had to end.

FOURTEEN

New Viewpoint

NOEL HAD TO LEAVE BY TEN O'CLOCK THE following morning. Still, there was time for a leisurely Sunday breakfast, with a chance for talk and an opportunity for Marcy's parents and Noel to get acquainted. Marcy sensed that Mom and Dad liked him and were impressed by his personality and mature manner. And he seemed equally drawn to them, which made her proud and pleased.

Afterward, she and Noel went for a necessarily brief drive around town. Marcy showed him the high school and a few other points of interest. It was really for a chance to talk with her alone, she suspected, that he had proposed the excursion.

He asked, as they turned back toward Marcy's house once more, "Will you be coming out to Colorado next summer?"

Marcy hardly knew how to answer, "Gee, I don't know, Noel. It depends on so many things—whether

Liz wants to, whether we get invited to the ranch, whether my parents would let me."

"How do you feel about it?" Noel asked, his hazel glance serious for a moment on her face. "Would you like to?"

"I—think so." Marcy's tone was a little choked.

Noel's eyes returned to the road ahead, but she could see his grin. He said, "I don't want to hurry you. You're still just a kid. I should have realized that last summer —only somehow I didn't. But don't forget me, Marcy. I can't seem to forget you, although I've been tryin'. I've gone around with some other girls."

"Cindy?" Marcy asked softly. She remembered the way Cindy Bayliss' dark, wistful glance had clung to Noel when he wasn't looking her way or paying any attention to her.

But Noel shook his head. "Not Cindy. We used to have kind of a case on each other when we were in high school, but I got over it quite a while back. Cindy took longer, but now she's goin' steady with Mark Hayward —you remember him, don't you? A big blond fella with curly hair?"

Marcy nodded. It all seemed long ago now, but Noel's words brought back to life the people she had met at the Lazy K, the things they had done, the places they'd seen. She was glad Cindy had found someone else. Still, Marcy thought, it isn't really fair for me to try to keep Noel dangling.

She said, "I don't know what to tell you, Noel. I still like you a lot. But I'm very fond of Steve, too. I can't seem to make up my mind yet about—about—"

"Take it easy," Noel grinned. "I'm not tryin' to pin

you down. I know you're only seventeen and girls around these parts don't seem to grow up as fast as they do out west. I've been tryin' to tell myself that what happened to us last summer was just one of those vacation romances, or whatever you want to call 'em. But now that I've seen you again—well, I'm still not sure. Is it like that with you, too?"

Marcy could only nod, afraid to trust her voice.

Noel said, "Tell you what—we'll let it ride and see how things shape up later on. I figured I might never get to see you again, but here we are together. You can't tell what may happen. So just don't forget me. File me away somewhere in the back of your mind for future reference. And I'll do the same."

Marcy's smile was tremulous, agreeing. "I guess that's all we can do." But she thought, Only I'm afraid I'll file you in the back of my heart, instead of my mind . . .

When Noel had been gone a day or so, it was as though he had never been to Westfield at all. Marcy's life resumed its regular pattern. The routine of schoolwork and housework hadn't changed, and yet, Marcy realized, something was different. She tried to decide what it was and finally came to the conclusion that it was her own attitude.

She told Liz one morning as they walked to school, "I never really believed there was anything to the idea that your frame of mind could affect what happened to you. Now I don't know. It seemed," she went on, smiling a little at her friend's puzzled look, "that all the time I felt so down in the dumps and sorry for myself— well, nothing exciting happened to me, nothing worked out the way I wanted it to. And then I'd just brood more than ever. But since Thanksgiving I've kind of snapped out of it. So what happens? Noel pops up."

Liz nodded. "That was a break," she admitted. "But he's gone again now."

"I know," Marcy said. "But something else happened yesterday." In order to tell Liz about it, she would have to explain Ken's theory and her own promise to give it a try. This Marcy proceeded to do.

"And you mean," Liz demanded, her eyes wide with interest, "you've actually experimented and it worked?"

Marcy smiled. "It was funny in a way," she said reminiscently. "As we were gathering up our books to leave study hall, I noticed that Rick had one of those program booklets from the Stock Show. I wasn't even thinking about Ken's theory when I asked if he'd been to the exposition. And Rick said yes. So then I told him I had, too, and we got to talking about it. He walked me all the way to my next class. He's awfully keen on horses and when I told him I'd ridden quite a lot when we were out west last summer, he asked if I'd come out to his folks' place—they live about three miles out of town— some Saturday and go riding."

"Well, blow me down!" Liz said. Her enjoyment of the horses on her uncle's ranch hadn't begun to equal Marcy's. "I'll settle for a car any time, myself. But if your and Rick's common fondness for horses leads to a real date—"

"Not so fast," Marcy broke in, laughing. "But at least, we're going riding next Saturday." She went on, "And he's not nearly as hard to talk with as you thought he'd be. He's not quiet at all when you talk about something he's interested in."

Liz shook her head. "It looks like your clever brother had the right idea after all. You haven't seemed so intrigued with a boy for ages—not with any boy who's available, that is . . ."

On Saturday Rick Whitney, looking taller and thinner than ever in Levi's and a plaid lumberjack shirt, drove up to the Rhodes's house in an old station wagon to pick Marcy up. Marcy, too, wore jeans and lumberjack and she had tied a wool scarf over her head against the nip of the chill wind. But it was a bright sunny day and, according to Rick, perfect for riding.

They drove out to a rambling, white-painted country house, with a towering red barn behind it, and a three-rail rustic fence edging the grounds.

"We don't really farm," Rick explained in his shy, rather hesitant way. "We just like living in the country. My father commutes to Clay City to work. We've only got two horses, one for my kid sister and one for me. You'll ride Beverly's."

"Won't she mind?" Marcy asked, walking toward the barn with Rick.

He shook his head. "It's all set. Bev has to go to dancing class in town Saturday mornings. My mother took her in. Dad's probably out around the barn somewhere."

Marcy met Rick's father, a tall, thin, graying counterpart of Rick himself. He talked with Marcy and Rick in quiet, friendly fashion as he helped saddle the bay mare that Marcy would ride and the big roan gelding which was Rick's. He opened the gate at the back of the pasture and waved to them as they cantered off briskly down the winding country road.

It was a wonderful ride. The wind was cold in their faces but the sun warmed their backs. The bay responded well and Marcy liked the powerful surge of the muscular body under her, the even rhythm of the horse's gait. Rick's horse kept going ahead whenever they let their mounts out. But when they turned back toward the Whitney farm, they held their horses to a walk and moved along side by side, talking.

Marcy said, "I haven't ridden since last summer. I'm surprised I haven't forgotten how."

But Rick told her, "It isn't a thing you forget. You ride well, as if you really enjoy it."

"Oh, I do," Marcy said. "But I expect it sort of cramped your style, having to keep slowing down and waiting for me."

"It's just that my horse is more spirited," Rick said. And he added, "This has been fun. I don't know anyone else who likes to ride—except Bev and she's not much good. She's only thirteen—and besides, she's my sister."

Marcy laughed and they got to discussing brothers and sisters. She told him about Ken and how much she missed him. Then, through some indirect connection, they drifted on to the subject of the school paper, to which both of them had contributed material on occasion.

"What I really like to write," Marcy heard herself admitting, quite to her own surprise, "is poetry. Not that I'm very good," she amended hastily, feeling color flare up in her face. Now why had she confided a thing like that to Rick Whitney?

She cast a quick glance at him, jogging along beside her, expecting to see him smile. But he said quite seriously, "You do? That's funny. So do I. I'll bet my stuff isn't as good as yours, though. But I like fooling around with words and meter—and I love to read poetry."

Marcy nodded in agreement, surprised and intrigued by this unexpected discovery of a shared interest. Ken had been right, she thought fleetingly, when he said you had to get to know a person a little in order to learn whether you liked him or not. She could have gone on indefinitely, sitting next to Rick in study hall, without finding out anything personal about him at all. Now, in a few hours spent together, they were on the verge of becoming friends.

Rather to Marcy's surprise, Rick dropped in the very next evening to bring her a book of poetry he had particularly enjoyed. And he lingered to talk awhile and to have a cup of hot chocolate in front of the fireplace with Marcy and her parents. When she saw him to the door he asked her rather diffidently to go to the movies with him on Wednesday night and Marcy accepted.

"Such a nice boy," Mom said, when Marcy came smiling back into the living room. She asked then, her blue glance inquiring, "You are having more fun lately, aren't you, dear?"

Marcy nodded, admitting, "Even a little attention from a boy—well, it does something for a girl. And Rick is interesting when you get to know him." She went on, feeling a sudden urge to confide in her parents, "I was in such a rut for a while this fall. But Ken gave me a talking-to when he was home. And my viewpoint seems to have changed. I don't know what was the matter with me before."

Dad told her, "We were afraid it was your mother's going back to work that had thrown you."

But Marcy shook her head in quick denial. "I was all churned up inside before that happened," she said. "Feeling sorry for myself because Steve was gone, unhappy about our old crowd scattering. I just couldn't seem to get adjusted to things as they are this year. But I've got a little more sense now."

"You've always had plenty of sense," her mother insisted staunchly. "It wasn't too easy a situation to adjust to. And then my going back to nursing complicated things still more, threw a lot of extra work on your shoulders."

"Not enough to hurt me any," Marcy said. "I guess the trouble was, I thought of myself too much at first. I couldn't seem to see anyone else's side of things. Actually," she told Mom, "you have it lots harder than I."

"But I'm doing something I want to do," her mother pointed out, "something I chose myself. That makes a difference. Even when I'm tired and my feet hurt, I have a sense of satisfaction in my job, of accomplishment. But taking care of things at home—well, that's not the sort of work that has much appeal for a girl your age."

"It's not so bad," Marcy grinned. "And look at the practice I'm getting."

She could tell, by their expressions, that her parents

were proud of her. And the realization made her feel warm and happy. It also made her aware that this might be an especially propitious time to bring up a subject that had been nagging at the back of her mind for several days.

"Uh—I was just wondering about something," Marcy began, her glance going hopefully from one parent to the other. "The Firehouse Follies is next Saturday."

Mom nodded, a faint smile tugging at her lips. "And you'd like a new formal?" she asked.

"You must be psychic," Marcy said in surprise.

Dad chuckled. "Didn't you know that we parents develop a sort of sixth sense that warns us when the subject of a new formal is about to be broached?" He smiled over at Mom, adding, "I think a college week end calls for one, don't you, Lila?"

"Definitely," Mom agreed.

As Marcy had often thought before, they were really very nice parents.

❧ FIFTEEN ❧

Marcy's Older Man

MARCY, WITH LIZ'S HELP, BEGAN SHOPPING
for a formal the very next day after school. This was a
delicate and usually a time-consuming process, but for
once they found exactly what Marcy had hoped for in
the first shop they went to, a dress so delectable and becoming that its effect on Steve, or any other young male,
was bound to be cataclysmic. Marcy took it home on
approval, since she was practically certain her mother
would fall in love with its soft melon color and artful
lines, just as she and Liz had.

"It's simply beautiful," Mom said, her eyes shining,
as Marcy modeled it for her and Dad that evening.
"The color is perfect with your hair and that draped
bodice—"

Dad interrupted doubtfully, "Isn't it a little—" But
he broke off whatever he had been about to say and,
instead, finished with an admiring grin, "Well, no, I
guess not. After all, I have to remember how grown up

you're getting, baby. And that's quite a dress. As Ken would say if he were here—'wow!' "

Coming from her father, Marcy thought that was one of the nicest compliments she had ever received.

"I'm glad you both like it," she said. "I know it cost a little bit more than we usually pay. But I figured it will still be perfectly good for a dance at school, if someone asks me, because no one at high will have seen it."

"What do you mean, *if* someone asks you?" Dad demanded. "How about that young fellow who was here last night?"

He sounded so belligerent that Marcy had to smile. "Rick isn't too keen on dancing," she said. "But don't worry. All I can think of now is the Firehouse Follies."

She went up to her room then to change her clothes and hang the exciting new dress carefully away on a padded hanger in her closet. It made her old formals look limp and dowdy by comparison. Marcy smoothed them down surreptitiously, so that they wouldn't feel too inadequate. They, too, had sparkled with brand-new loveliness in their day.

When she joined her parents in the living room once more, her mother was saying, "—never felt so sorry for anyone before. He hasn't had a single visitor all the weeks he's been there."

"Who?" Marcy demanded, touched.

"Mr. Tuttle," her mother said. "I guess he hasn't any family. And he told me he's so old all his friends are dead."

"How awful!" Marcy exclaimed, feeling pity stir in her even more deeply. "What happened to him? What's he in the hospital for?"

"He broke his leg," Mom explained. "He slipped on a scatter rug in the big old house where he lives all alone. And I guess it was almost two days before his calls for help were heard, so he was in pretty bad shape when he was brought in. He's doing all right now, except that at his age it takes bones forever to knit. He's sort of a cantankerous old character—but I like him. I stick my head into the room to say hello whenever I'm on duty on his floor. He's really pathetic. He hates television and his eyesight isn't good enough for him to read a lot. So you know what he does to keep occupied? Figures out chess problems."

"Chess?" Dad repeated. "All by himself? Too bad he hasn't got a crony to play with."

Mom nodded. "That's what I told him. But he said he hadn't. And then he asked sort of wistfully if I didn't play, or if I knew anyone who did." She smiled at Marcy. "I admitted that I didn't have the brain for it, but that both my children played some. He asked me to bring them in, but I explained about Ken being away at college and you being too busy."

Marcy nodded. She was too busy, of course. Still, the idea of poor old Mr. Tuttle figuring out chess plays all by himself made her throat ache a bit.

When they were getting ready to go upstairs to bed an hour or so later, the thought of the old man still haunted Marcy. She asked her mother, "Do you suppose he'd really get any kick out of playing with anyone as young as I? I'm pretty rusty, too. Ken and I used to play a lot, but I haven't even thought about chess in ages."

Her mother laid her hand on Marcy's shoulder. "Honey, don't let it bother you. I was just telling Dad about him because I feel sorry for the poor old fellow. But I didn't mean—"

"But would he?" Marcy persisted. "If you think he'd like it, I could spend an evening playing chess with him once in a while. Tomorrow night for instance. I'm not doing a thing."

Her mother smiled at her and her eyes looked very bright. But all she said was, "He'd love it, I know. Shall I tell him you'll be there?"

Marcy nodded and the pitying ache in her throat stopped bothering her so much . . .

She played chess with Mr. Tuttle two evenings that week. After all, Marcy felt, it wasn't much trouble to drive to the hospital at seven and keep the old man occupied until visiting hours were over at nine. He was a weazened little figure on the high white bed, the mound made by his plaster cast under the covers seeming the biggest thing about him. He reminded Marcy of the seven dwarfs in the Disney version of *Snow White,* a sort of composite of Grumpy and Doc. But his gruffness melted long before their first evening together was over. Marcy suspected it was a sort of shield behind which he sought to hide his loneliness and eagerness for companionship. He beat her soundly at their first game, then seemed struck by anxiety for fear she wouldn't want to play again.

But Marcy felt no shame over her defeat. "You're an expert," she accused, smiling. "I can tell I'm out of my class."

"Nothing of the sort!" he denied sharply. "I was just lucky." She caught a gleam of apprehension in his eyes.

"You'll have to teach me the finer points," she tried to reassure him, "or I can't ever make it interesting for you."

"I'll do that," he told her quickly. "You'll beat me yet. Anyway, it's the game that counts, not who wins." He asked then, his old voice wistfully hopeful, "Will you play again soon?"

Marcy hesitated, pondering. There was her date the following night with Rick Whitney. Then she'd have to begin to get ready for the wonderful week end at Steve's college. But next week she shouldn't be so busy. She suggested, "How about Thursday?"

"This Thursday?" Mr. Tuttle's eyes lit with shining expectancy. "Day after tomorrow?"

Marcy opened her mouth to say she'd meant next week. But she just didn't have the heart to disappoint the beaming little old man. Instead, she nodded, smiling. She'd manage somehow.

When Marcy came back on Thursday, Mr. Tuttle greeted her like an old friend. He'd got one of the nurses to buy him a big box of chocolates and these he pressed on Marcy hospitably as they played. She felt she must warn him she couldn't always come to see him so often. But she took the sting out of it by promising, "I'll come once a week, though, at least. You can count on that."

"What night?" Mr. Tuttle asked eagerly. "Just so's I can figure ahead. Any time you say," he chuckled drily, and added. "I'm not swamped with social engagements."

"Thursday," Marcy told him, after a moment's

thought. "I'll make it oftener when I can. But we'll call it a regular weekly date every Thursday."

When the warning bell rang for the end of visiting hours, Marcy put away the chess board and told Mr. Tuttle good night. She went out into the tiled corridor along which visitors were emerging from various rooms to mingle with white-clad nurses on their way to settle their patients comfortably for the night.

Marcy paused at the top of the stairs to put on her coat. Just as she was shrugging into it, she felt a hand helping her pull it up and glanced around in surprise. Her eyes widened still more at the sight of Bruce Douglas standing there, grinning down at her.

"Hi, Marcy," he greeted her. "What are you doing here?"

Marcy smiled back at him, murmuring, "Hi, yourself. I could ask you the same question."

As they moved together down the broad stairway, she thought quizzically, Did you imagine I only existed in English class, or the corridor at high, because those are the only places you ever see me?

Bruce told her, "I was over at a fellow's house near here. So I dropped by to try to bum a ride home with my father. But he'll be tied up in surgery for another hour, so I guess I walk."

"I could give you a lift," Marcy offered impulsively. "I've got our car downstairs."

"Gee, that'd be swell," Bruce told her in his friendly fashion. "I guess it wouldn't take you much out of your way to drop me off. And I'd appreciate it."

Marcy said, as he held the heavy outer door for her,

"I didn't realize your father was a doctor. My mother's a nurse here."

"She is?" Bruce asked. "I didn't know that, either. Were you here to see her?"

Marcy shook her head, smiling, pulling up her coat collar against the bite of the wind. As they crossed the parking lot to her car, she explained about Mr. Tuttle. And Bruce seemed interested. He proved talkative and easy as they drove along. It was funny, Marcy thought fleetingly, when you figured that they'd sat near each other in class for months without exchanging more than a few casual words. Now, having run into each other outside that familiar environment, they were yakking away like old friends.

"How about a Coke?" she was surprised to hear Bruce suggest as they drew near the Sweet Shop.

"Why—okay," Marcy said, "if you like."

It was exciting to walk into the brightly lit, half-filled room with one of the most popular boys at school. Classmates hailed Bruce from every side, including Marcy in their jovial greetings. There was a touch of envy, Marcy noted, too, in several girls' looks. She couldn't help smiling just a little at the realization. So far as the others knew, she might have had a regular date with Bruce Douglas, they might be stopping for something to eat after the early movie. Marcy's chin lifted just a little in proud pleasure at the reflected glory that was hers because of her association with the tall, good-looking boy beside her. She knew he was only buying her a Coke because she'd been kind enough to give him a lift home. But the others didn't, so she might as well enjoy the situation to the fullest. Marcy said a small inaudible thank you to Mr. Tuttle for his unconscious share in bringing this moment about.

The following day in English, when Bruce said his customary, "Hi" to Marcy as he sat down beside her, she thought his smile wasn't quite so impersonal as usual. Maybe she imagined the change, but she didn't think so. And he leaned over once to ask her some question about an assignment. And as the final bell rang and they rose to leave, he inquired, grinning, "You going to see Mr. Tuttle again tonight?"

Marcy shook her head, smiling, too, feeling excitement rise in her. "Not tonight. It's Friday and I've got to pack."

"Pack?" Bruce's brows rose questioningly. "You going away somewhere?"

Marcy's smile widened and her eyes shone with happy anticipation. "I'm going to Carveth College for the week end. There's a big fraternity dance."

Bruce pursed his lips in a practically silent whistle. "Some fun!" he exclaimed, grinning. Was there a new touch of respect in his manner, Marcy wondered, or did she imagine that, too? "Have yourself a time. I'll have to hear all the details Monday."

As they separated at the door to go their respective ways, he gave her elbow a little friendly squeeze as he said, "Be seeing you. Don't forget to come back."

"Oh, I won't." Marcy smiled at him.

Liz, who had been waiting for her in the corridor glanced from Marcy to Bruce Douglas' tall figure striding off down the hall, then back once more to her friend. Her lips were parted just a little in astonishment. "Since when," she demanded softly, "have you two been on such friendly terms?"

"Oh, it doesn't mean anything," Marcy told her. But it was nice to have Liz looking at her in such an impressed way. "Come on." Marcy tucked her arm through her friend's. "I'll tell you all about it as we walk to class . . ."

SIXTEEN

Firehouse Follies

IT DIDN'T SEEM TO MARCY THAT SHE HAD A
chance to catch her breath the next morning, until she
was settled on the train, waving good-bye to her father
through the wide window. Behind her was the mad rush
of getting ready, of dropping Mom off at the hospital, of
driving with Dad over to Clay City in time for the ten-
o'clock train. Now, with some four hours of travel
stretching ahead, Marcy drew a deep breath and relaxed
for a blissful interval of anticipation.

Just what would a college week end be like, she wondered? The dance she could partially imagine, from
things Ken and Steve had told her about it. But Steve's
recent letters had mentioned an informal party at the
Student Union this afternoon, to be followed by dinner
at a restaurant in town with Ken and his girl, Lee Creighton. Then, after Chapel Sunday morning there would
be a brunch at the fraternity house. "And from then
on," Steve had written, "I plan to keep you all to myself

133

till I have to see you aboard the three o'clock train for home."

Delicious little shivers of excitement wandered up and down Marcy's spine at the prospect. It all sounded so terrific she could scarcely wait for it to begin. But overshadowing all else was her sense of thrilled expectancy at the thought of seeing Steve again, of spending almost two whole days in his company.

"And we aren't going to quarrel," Marcy told herself firmly, staring out at the snowy countryside sweeping past the window. "I won't spoil things as I nearly did Thanksgiving."

If she met Thea, Marcy's thoughts continued, she would be perfectly friendly. It was very silly and childish to be jealous and she was over all that. She didn't expect to like the other girl, but she was certainly civilized enough to pretend she did. After all, Marcy felt, she could afford to be magnanimous. Steve had invited her to the dance, when he could have taken Thea with half the trouble. She guessed that proved whom he liked best.

Marcy was looking forward to meeting Lee Creighton, at whose sorority house arrangements had been made for her to stay. This should give her a real taste of college living, a sample of the way things would be next year, when she came to Carveth as a student, instead of a mere visitor. In a haze of such pleasant reflections, the hours on the train slipped away.

Steve was awaiting her on the station platform, along with numerous other expectant B Z's all craning their necks for a glimpse of the girls they were importing for the big week end. With Steve's cry of greeting in her ears, the feel of his arms catching her close in a welcoming hug, it seemed to Marcy that she stepped into a shining special world where excitement crackled in the air like electricity. There was a flattering note of pride in Steve's voice as he presented a couple of fraternity brothers to Marcy. And she couldn't help feeling that she looked as smooth and well-turned out as any of the other girls descending from the train. Her smart gray suit and bright red topcoat, her little gray hat with its crimson feather, helped build up within her a sense of well-being and self-confidence. And these in turn made it easy for her to talk with Steve's friends, to take part in all the joking and laughter.

"So this is Beezee!" Marcy exclaimed, as they all piled into the resplendent old fire truck waiting at the curb.

"The old girl herself," Steve chuckled. He went on to explain that the unconventional vehicle would transport all the visiting girls to the sorority houses and residence halls where they were to stay. Beezee would also serve to take them, as well as the college girls who had been invited, to the dance that night.

"But how can you crowd us all in?" Marcy asked.

"Oh, it takes several trips," Steve told her. "A dozen or so of the brothers go out, pick up their dates and bring them back to the B Z house. Then another dozen takes over and repeats the process. Just wait and you'll see how it works."

Several other imports beside Marcy were to stay at the Psi Delt house. Steve left her in the capable charge of Lee Creighton, a slim blonde, in plaid pedal-pushers and a white leather jacket, who came out to the fire truck to welcome Marcy. From their first glimpse of each other,

Marcy felt drawn to Ken's girl, with her crinkle-nosed smile and candid blue eyes. And Lee apparently liked Marcy, too. She led her up to the crowded, untidy little room they were to share and said, waving an airy hand about, "Welcome to Creighton Manor. It's only slightly larger than a phone booth, as you can see, but it's cozy."

"I hope I'm not putting you out," Marcy murmured, eyeing the single bed dubiously.

Lee laughed, a throaty little gurgle of sound, and indicated the studio couch, half-hidden under a drift of clothes and books and miscellany. "That's a bed, too, so there's plenty of room. Of course, it'll be a bit thick when we're dressing. But I wanted you to stay with me, or I wouldn't have asked you."

They had ample opportunity to get acquainted during the next hour or so. Ken and Steve picked them up at four for the short walk across the campus to the Student Union. The Open House was held in the big comfortable lounge, but the boys and Lee took Marcy for a complete tour of the building. Strolling along the wide corridors, her hand in Steve's, Marcy was duly impressed with all the beauties and facilities of the place. There were rooms upstairs for visiting parents, bowling alleys in the basement, club rooms, a refreshment bar and the wood-paneled central lounge.

Marcy kept thinking ecstatically, "Next year. Next year, I'll really feel at home here, I'll be a part of all this."

It seemed almost too wonderful to imagine.

Marcy met so many of Steve's and Ken's and Lee's friends at the Open House she was sure she'd never be able to remember all the names, or associate them with the right faces. But it was fun just the same. There was good talk and laughter as they all sat on the deep chairs and couches, or just stood about, eating their little cakes and drinking tea or coffee.

Later, over dinner in a dim-lit restaurant, apparently a favorite gathering spot of the college crowd, Marcy sat with Steve and Ken and Lee at a little corner table and talked and laughed some more. She felt too excited to eat much, although the food was good. It seemed so right to be with Steve again, to feel his liking and admiration wrapping her about like a warm cloak, to detect the gleam in his glance as their eyes caught and held.

"Gee, I've missed you," he murmured, his lips near her ear as Lee and Ken embarked on a private discussion of their own.

"I've missed you, too," Marcy admitted.

And it was true, just as true, really, as it had been at Thanksgiving time. The other boys she had met, the things she had done, even her brief re-encounter with Noel seemed to recede in importance when she was with Steve. But now when he asked, "What have you been doing?" she wasn't embarrassed and speechless. There were many things that had happened in the past weeks about which she could tell him. And Steve listened with interest and told her things he'd been doing. This ease between them made for easy conversation, for a feeling of closeness and understanding.

"It sounds," Ken broke in, his glance on Marcy, "as though you've been pretty busy since Thanksgiving."

"Oh, I have," Marcy told him and their eyes flashed a private message to each other. "I've met some new friends, done lots of things, had fun."

"That's the stuff," Ken grinned at her.

"Just don't go having too much fun," Steve admonished drily. "Not till I get home for the holidays."

The period after dinner, when the boys had left Marcy and Lee at the sorority house, passed in a mad rush and scramble of getting ready for the dance. The Psi Delt house resounded with shrieks of dismay over stocking runs or a misplaced earring, with near-hysterical laughter, with the rush and roar of showers and the beguiling voices of girls come borrowing. And such borrowing—everything from jewelry to nail polish to petticoats.

"Nothing's your own around here," Lee told Marcy, "so long as somebody thinks she can finagle you out of it. Might as well get used to the situation. You'll be in the thick of it yourself next year."

Marcy sighed happily, zipping up her lovely new formal, twisting this way and that for a satisfactory glimpse of it in the long mirror on Lee's closet door.

"What a perfectly zooty dress!" Lee exclaimed.

"Thanks," Marcy smiled at her. "Yours is awfully pretty, too."

"This little number?" Lee fluffed out the aqua net skirt that swirled from her off-the-shoulder black velvet bodice. "It's been made over so often I can't even remember how it was in the beginning. First I made a new top for the skirt and then a new skirt for the top—oh, well," she broke off with her little throaty laugh, "when you're going to college on a shoestring, you can't be choosy."

"You made it," Marcy inquired wonderingly, "yourself?"

"Doesn't it show?" Lee asked, laughing.

Marcy shook her head. "It's very smart."

"Well, good," Lee said. "Then I'm a success." She went on to explain, the while she applied her nail polish, "You see, my mother got a job to help put me through college. It's been kind of a struggle for her and Dad. I mean to make it up to them later on by helping my brother get educated when I'm through school and working. But in the meantime, my clothes budget is strictly from hunger and I sew a lot to stretch it. But Ken doesn't care, bless him."

"Neither do I," Marcy said. "I think you're swell!"

Lee gave her a little approving pat on the shoulder. And just then a carrying voice called from the hallway, "Step on it, you two. Your men are downstairs . . ."

Marcy knew she'd never forget the Firehouse Follies, not if she lived to be a hundred. It was like no dance she had ever gone to. There was the ride through the town streets in the old firetruck, siren wailing, crowded in cozily with Steve and Lee and Ken and eight or ten other couples. Then, when they reached the fraternity house, Marcy discovered that the guests must enter by climbing a ladder that extended from the street level to a window opening on a landing halfway between the first and second floors. She ascended hilariously with the others. Inside the house the fire theme had been carried out in every respect. Red fire helmets were suspended from the ceiling over the dance floor, huge cardboard cutouts of firemen carrying beautiful girls adorned the corners, and scorched lengths of burlap were hung at the windows. Climaxing all else was the knee-high smoke screen, which the boys explained had been caused by putting dry ice in water. This clung to the floor, giving the dancers an eerie out-of-this-world appearance as they moved to the orchestra's rhythms.

Marcy and Lee exclaimed enthusiastically over all the effects. "How did you think of them?" Marcy demanded.

Steve grinned, "The decorations committee really knocked itself out."

And Ken added regretfully, "We wanted to put in a fire pole and have everybody slide down it to get to the refreshment room in the basement. But it would have meant cutting a hole in the floor, so we couldn't."

"I'm just as glad," Lee murmured, and Marcy nodded in agreement.

On this very special, once-a-year occasion, the college authorities had granted the B Z's a three o'clock permission. This meant that when the dancing wound up at two, there was still time for breakfasting in the fraternity house dining room on scrambled eggs and some of the cook's justly famous hot biscuits. Food had never tasted better. And afterwards, Steve and Marcy strolled home across the quiet, dark campus, with Lee and Ken equally intent on each other somewhere on ahead.

Marcy told Steve, "It's been perfectly wonderful."

"You were wonderful," Steve said softly. "I never saw you look prettier. Gee, Marce, it'll be great next year when you're here all the time."

"What about Thea?" Marcy couldn't resist teasing.

But Steve pulled her close and kissed her in the deeper shadow of a tree near the Psi Delt porch. "Does that answer your question?" His voice was husky.

The pounding of Marcy's heart unsteadied her words a little, as she answered, "I don't care if you date her,

Steve. Honestly, I don't. I realize I was pretty silly Thanksgiving."

"So was I," Steve said, "to let you pick a fight the way I did. I should have appreciated your being jealous instead of getting sore about it."

"But I'm not jealous any more," Marcy told him. And it was practically true. "I met Thea tonight when Lee and I were getting dressed. She came in to bring back something of Lee's she'd borrowed. But I thought maybe she wanted a look at me, too."

"Oh?" Steve's tone was noncommittal.

Marcy went on, "I think she resented me, maybe, but she wasn't unpleasant about it or anything. She wasn't going to the dance. I found myself feeling a little sorry for her."

"She gets to go to plenty of dances," Steve said. He began then to talk about plans for the next day and Marcy sensed that he wanted to drop the subject of Thea. And that was all right with her, too.

Presently Lee said, her voice low and not far distant in the darkness, "I hate to break in on you two, but the hour grows late and our house mother's fussy about late permissions."

"Yeah," Ken backed her up, "Steve and I have to get going, too. You're not parting forever. Tomorrow's another day."

But not so wonderful as this one, Marcy thought, as her lips and Steve's met in a good night kiss. No other day could be.

SEVENTEEN

Week Before Christmas

AFTER CHAPEL THE NEXT MORNING STEVE took Marcy to his fraternity house again, but this time its Firehouse Follies aspect was entirely changed. Gone were the ladder and gaudy posters, the fire helmets and burlap drapes and smoke screen. Miraculously the place had assumed a tastefully decorated look of neatness and order.

"It looks as if you've been busy little bees," Marcy said, glancing around appreciatively.

"We worked like dogs," Steve said simply, "every last one of us. Got up an hour earlier than we usually have to for Chapel."

"And twenty-nine guys" Ken added, "working for one hour is the equivalent of one guy working twenty-nine hours."

"I think you're all wonderful," Marcy assured Ken. But her glance told Steve he was the most wonderful of all.

142

Brunch was delicious waffles and fat pork sausages, served at the long tables in the dining-room. The cook, plump and gray-haired and beaming, came in to take a bow and the boys sang her an admiring serenade. Everyone lingered when the meal was over, talking and laughing and joined in on the choruses of college songs. The B Z's harmonized on a group of fraternity songs, frankly sentimental, but sweet and moving just the same. Marcy felt thrilled by the surging upswell of male voices and happy to be a part of it all, accumulating memories that would stay with her always.

It was nearly noon when the gay party broke up. Outside, the chill fresh air felt good against Marcy's face. The sky was a clear soft blue and the bright sunshine had melted all the snow except for a few white ruffles edging the sidewalks.

"What would you like to do now?" Steve asked. "Go for a walk? Head over to the Union? There's always something doing there."

"Let's walk," Marcy said. "Show me all the places you've mentioned in your letters. The Library and Todd Hall and—oh, everyplace."

Steve grinned down at her and she realized she had chosen what he'd rather do, too. "Sure you won't be cold?"

Marcy shook her head, pulling her scarlet coat more closely about her as Steve tucked his hand through her arm.

They walked along the winding campus paths, past the places Marcy had mentioned and many others. But they paid a good deal more attention to each other than to the buildings they passed. The old magic of their liking for each other wove its familiar spell. They talked or were silent as the spirit moved them. And Steve caught her close and kissed her, in the little sheltered pocket behind the imposing monument of old Merriwether Carveth, 1810——1893. There was a tradition, he explained gravely, about kissing your girl behind the statue. "And we can't fly in the face of tradition," he pointed out.

Marcy's smile was a bit unsteady. "I suppose not—but this could get to be habit forming."

"Can't think of a nicer habit," Steve said. And he gave Merriwether's foot an appreciative pat as they walked away.

Where the time went, Marcy simply couldn't imagine. But Steve got her back to the Psi Delt house and to a slightly worried Lee barely in time to pack.

"We only took a walk," Marcy explained apologetically, as Lee helped her fold and put things into her suitcase with the ease of long practice. "I don't know how it got so late."

Lee's smile was knowing. "Time does get away from you. But you'll make your train all right."

Marcy had only a moment to thank Lee for her hospitality as they hurried downstairs. "You've been grand to me."

Lee kissed her cheek. "Don't mention it. I had fun, too. Come again any time."

Steve had borrowed a car to take Marcy to the station. They drove off quickly, leaving Lee and Ken waving good-bye from the sorority house steps. By the time they reached their destination, there were only a couple of minutes until train time. All about them fraternity brothers of Steve's were bidding their girls good-bye. And just then Steve remembered belatedly and with some chagrin that he had forgotten to take Marcy to lunch.

"I'll never miss it," Marcy assured him, "not after all those waffles." She tried to thank Steve, to tell him what a marvelous time she'd had. But he was thanking her for coming and telling her how much he'd enjoyed it. Before they got the matter half settled, Marcy's train arrived.

Steve's last words, as he stood there looking up at her from the station platform, were, "Remember now, I'll be home in less than a week."

As if she could forget anything so wonderful, Marcy thought, waving good-bye to him . . .

There were only three days of school that week. Then the Christmas holidays would start. Marcy moved through the brief interval in a happy daze, filled with glowing memories of the week end just past, with bright expectations for the immediate future. Liz had to hear all about Marcy's stay at Carveth, of course, and repeating every detail made them stand out even more clearly in Marcy's mind.

"Some people have all the luck," Liz said wistfully. "I haven't been to a single college week end."

"You will sometime," Marcy assured her. "You'll be in college yourself next year."

"That's not the same," Liz said. "But anyway, I'm glad it happened to you, so I could enjoy it secondhand."

Marcy's parents, too, were interested in hearing about all the fun she'd had. While Marcy and her mother wrapped Christmas gifts at the dining table and Dad sat nearby lending moral support and making admiring comments on their handiwork, she described the activities of the week end for them.

When she had finished, Dad inquired, frowning, "But didn't you have any dates with anyone but Steve?"

Marcy glanced up at him in wide-eyed astonishment. "Why—of course not! He invited me."

"It's different nowadays, George," Mom explained, fluffing up the silver bow she had just tied.

"What do you mean?" Marcy demanded. "How did it use to be?"

Mom smiled, a dreamy reminiscent little smile. And Dad said, "When I went to college, the girls we imported for dances wouldn't let us get away with any such monopoly. Not only did we have to compete with the whole stag line for their favors, but they expected us to arrange dates for them with our friends as well."

"They did?" Marcy repeated, slightly stunned at the idea.

Mom said, "It seems to me our college week ends were much more exciting. It was a whirl of new faces all the time. One boy would take you to breakfast, another for a walk, then back to your own beau for tea-dancing. Never a dull moment."

"I didn't have a dull moment, either," Marcy insisted. "Steve showed me a wonderful time."

Mom patted her hand. "I'm sure he did, dear."

And Dad added, with a little grin, "Other days, other customs. Sometimes I can't see that all the changes are improvements, though. But so long as you kids don't know what you're missing—" he left it at that.

Marcy glanced from one of her parents to the other thoughtfully. But neither of them was looking at her. Their glances were locked in a warmly personal look that made her feel happy, even though it excluded her. The fact that your parents loved and understood each other was a nice thing to know.

Very little work was done at school those last days before the holidays. There was quite a round of social activity. Several of the clubs held Christmas parties and Marcy went with Rick Whitney to the one given by the Journalism Club. It was an informal affair, held in the school Activities Room. But there were some amusing skits and games and everyone had a lot of fun.

Afterward, driving home with Rick, Marcy said happily, "I love this time of year, don't you? Everything seems special somehow. All the rush and excitement and people being nicer than usual to each other."

Rick nodded. "I like it, too." He asked then, "Will I get to see anything of you, though, when Steve Judson's home?" The wistful note in his tone touched Marcy. She really liked Rick. He was one of those reserved people who grew on you with acquaintance. She always had fun when they were together since so many of their tastes and interests were similar. And there was no denying that Rick's attention had done a lot to bolster up Marcy's self-esteem, to convince her that she was capable of attracting a boy if she cared to try. He could never take Steve's place with her, but Marcy didn't think he expected to. All he seemed to want was that their pleasant, easy friendship should continue. And she wanted this, too.

She told him, smiling a little, "I don't see why you shouldn't. Steve won't monopolize all my time."

"That's all I wanted to know." Rick grinned. "How about going to a movie with me tomorrow night?"

Marcy hesitated for only a second. Steve would be getting home tomorrow night. But he had written that he and Ken were driving with the same fraternity brother who had dropped them off before and wouldn't be arriving till after midnight.

"I'd love to," she told Rick, and meant it . . .

Usually, Lila Rhodes spent her day off at home, doing some job or other and taking the chore of meal preparation off Marcy's hands. But this particular Wednesday she had been invited to her bridge club's holiday luncheon party and Marcy had persuaded her to accept.

"You've missed so many meetings now," Marcy had pointed out when the subject first came up. "And the Christmas party's special. Go on and go. I don't mind."

Mom had still seemed dubious. "It doesn't seem fair to you, when I have so little time at home."

But Marcy had argued, putting an affectionate arm around her mother's shoulders, "Remember when you decided to go back to work, you said it would mean a three-way partnership for us all? That didn't mean much to me then. I felt grumpy about the whole deal and sort of abused. But I've honestly got over that. It doesn't even bother me to come home to an empty house any more. I've got too many other things to think about, more important things. I really feel like a partner now. And so why shouldn't you go to your bridge party? You wouldn't mind if I went out and left you with a little extra work sometime, would you?"

Her mother had smiled then, admitting, "Of course not. And I'll go, so long as that's the way you feel about it."

Her blue glance, so proud on Marcy's face, had said quite a bit more than that. But there was no need to put some things into words.

When Marcy got home from school that afternoon, her mother had long since left for her party. The house had a holiday look and feel about it, despite its emptiness and quiet. The big holly wreath on the front door, the drift of Christmas greens on the mantel, with tall red candles thrusting up among them, the mysterious packages which Marcy knew were tucked away in every closet, seemed to create an almost tangible excitement in the air.

Marcy was humming as she went upstairs to her room and the song she hummed was "Oh, Little Town of Bethlehem." Very appropriate, Marcy thought, smiling, with Christmas only a few days off. And no more school, she told herself. Two glorious weeks of vacation stretched enticingly ahead. And Steve would be home tomorrow.

If I were any happier, Marcy thought, I'd burst!

She took off her yellow sweater and pleated plaid skirt and changed into old blue jeans and a white tee-shirt. There was no work to do until time to start dinner, since Mildred had left the house spotless and shining yesterday. Marcy flipped on her little radio and sat down to do her nails. Just as she finished, the phone rang and it was Liz. So that took care of the next half hour. By that time, Marcy realized, she'd better get started on dinner. Mom might be late. Bridge club parties had a way of stretching out and Mom would have a lot of talk to catch up on with all her friends.

Marcy had the meat loaf and potatoes in the oven and was just getting salad ingredients out of the refrigerator when she heard the front door open. She glanced at the kitchen clock. Five-fifteen was too early for Dad. It must be Mom, getting in a bit sooner than Marcy had expected. But before she could call out a greeting, a much deeper and more masculine voice than Mom's shouted, "Anybody home around here?"

"Ken!" Marcy gasped, but she was so startled her voice scarcely came out at all. How could it be her brother at this hour?

And now another male voice—Steve's, Marcy's heart told her in a swift leap—added its comment to Ken's. "I smell something cooking. Somebody's here. Hey, Marce!"

Breathless with surprise, her eyes shining, Marcy flew to welcome them. But even as she ran, a small warning signal flashed in her mind. Here was Steve, back hours before she had expected him. Would he be planning to spend his first evening at home with his family? Or would he be expecting to take her out? And if he did have any such idea, what about her date with Rick?

Anyway you looked at it, Marcy realized fleetingly, here were all the ingredients that could add up to trouble.

❧ EIGHTEEN ❧

A Talk With Steve

STEVE AND KEN LOOKED BIG AND WONDER-
ful there in the front hall, bare-headed, their trench coats
belted casually, their grins wide. Marcy was struck anew
by how much more mature they seemed, how they had
changed in the months away at college. She couldn't
imagine a thing like that, could she? Her heart beat so
fast she could scarcely speak.

"You two!" she gasped as Ken caught her in a brief
bear hug. "We didn't expect you for hours yet."

"The powers that be changed their minds and let us
off at noon," Ken said, "so we got an early start."

"Move over, boy," Steve tapped Ken's shoulder. "She's
my girl." He held Marcy close for a moment and their
lips met. Words didn't seem necessary between them
at all.

Ken followed his nose tactfully out to the kitchen.
"Something smells good," he sniffed appreciatively.
"Dinner ready yet? I'm starved."

"Not quite," Marcy admitted when she and Steve came out to join him a moment later, "but almost. And Mom and Dad should be home pretty soon."

Ken opened the oven and peeked in. "Looks good, too. I hope you made plenty."

"Always enough for one more," Marcy smiled. But her glance went a shade apprehensively toward Steve.

He shook his head, apparently taking her look as an invitation. "I can't stay for dinner. My folks would have a fit if I didn't come home as long as I'm in town."

But before Marcy could do more than draw a relieved breath, he added, "I'll be back right afterward, though. As soon as I can make it."

"I'm sorry, Steve," her voice came out in a hoarse little rush, "but I've got a date tonight."

"A date?" Steve stared at her frowning. "Fine thing, my first night home."

"But you know I didn't expect you till tomorrow. That is, I figured if you didn't get here till midnight I wouldn't be seeing you till tomorrow."

"That's right, Steve," Ken said mildly. "We did kind of jump the gun, breezing in hours ahead of schedule."

"I suppose so," Steve agreed. "But I'm disappointed just the same."

"So am I," Marcy admitted.

Steve grinned down at her. "Well, in that case, I'll forgive you." He asked then, "You're free tomorrow night, I trust?"

"Well—" Marcy hesitated, "practically." At Steve's forbidding scowl, she hurried on, "I only have to spend a little time with Mr. Tuttle. You remember, I told you all about him last week end. He always expects me on Thursday, but I won't have to stay during the whole visiting period. I can get away by eight or eight-thirty easily. We can do something then."

"You're darn' right we can," Steve said, relaxing. "For a minute there, you had me scared. But so long as my rival's in his seventies, I guess I needn't worry."

"Of course not," Marcy said, with a little smile.

A sudden thought seemed to strike Steve. "Your date tonight's with someone younger, though, I take it?"

Marcy nodded. "Yes, it is."

Just then, the front door opened and her mother came in, to be followed only a few minutes later by her father. So there was no further chance for anything even remotely resembling private conversation between Marcy and Steve.

When he left a short while later, his manner was as cordial as it had been when he came, but Marcy noticed a rather quizzically curious gleam in his dark eyes. Still, she asked herself, why should she go out of her way to tell him with whom she was going out tonight? If he asked, she would do so. But otherwise—well, a little uncertainty was good for a man. Marcy had often heard Liz say so and she was inclined to agree.

Dinner was like old times, Marcy thought, as the four of them sat around the table in the dining room, catching up on all of each other's news. It was wonderful having Ken home again. The family had seemed incomplete without him. Now for two whole weeks the table would be balanced, Ken on one side, she on the other, as Marcy had grown up thinking it should be.

Their talk touched on one topic after another, some

light and casual, others serious. The foreign situation was grave, although it seemed strange even to think of war and horror in these pleasant surroundings. But there was always the realization hovering over the family that Ken might be drafted and have to drop his studies for a while. Marcy had often heard her parents discussing it while he was away. It could happen to Steve, too, she knew. Young men were being called into service every day and while Steve and Ken weren't yet nineteen, it wouldn't be long until they were. The thought gave her an unhappy qualm.

"Some of the fellows," Ken said, "figure they'll leave school after their freshman year and get their army hitch over. But I kind of lean toward the idea of waiting till they tap me."

Did Steve feel that way, too, Marcy wondered? She hoped so. This decision facing all the boys she knew wasn't an easy one to make.

Dad said, "I think you're right there. They'll take you when they need you."

And Mom added, with wistful optimism, "And maybe the world won't always be in such a mess that we have to have a big army."

Marcy found herself feeling sorry for her parents, for all parents. When a boy was called into service, it was like a pebble dropping into a stream. The circles widened, touching his family, the girl who cared for him, his friends. She tried to shut the thought away from her. Probably Ken and Mom and Dad were doing that, too. At least the tenor of their talk changed rather quickly and soon they were laughing again. It was well to laugh together while they could . . .

Steve came over the next morning while Marcy was doing the breakfast dishes. He even went so far as to dry them for her.

"Better watch that," Ken warned. "She'll start thinking she's got you all domesticated."

"No, I won't," Marcy denied. "I told him he didn't need to. But he's just naturally more considerate than you."

It was fun, kidding and laughing with the two of them and Marcy enjoyed it to the full. Afterward, they phoned Rosemary and cooked up a table tennis game at the Park House. They played several hot doubles, in which Marcy and Steve emerged the victors.

"Fine thing!" Ken mourned. "Get beaten by my own kid sister, just because I taught her how to play so well!"

"You should have concentrated on me," Rosemary said. "My game's awful."

"Have to take that in hand," Ken grinned, "while I'm home. We'll challenge these two to a return engagement after I get you in shape."

"We're not scared, are we, Marce?" Steve chuckled.

Marcy shook her head confidently. "I should say not. We'll take them on any time."

When they left the Park House, it had begun to snow. Great soft flakes were falling from the gray sky.

"Oh, good," Marcy said. "Just in time for Christmas."

"Doesn't seem possible," Rosemary murmured, "that it's only two days off."

"Hey!" Ken exclaimed. "It's almost one o'clock."

"No wonder I'm so hungry," Steve said. "Let's all stop at the Sweet Shop for a hamburger."

"And a malted," Ken elaborated, "and maybe some pie a la mode."

"Maybe," Rosemary suggested, "some more of the crowd will be there."

She proved quite right. At the Sweet Shop they ran into Liz, who was with Bill Weaver, just in from Texas and looking very tanned and handsome. Liz's eyes were bright and her manner enthusiastic.

"We've been looking for you," she told Marcy and the others. "I tried to phone but nobody answered. We want to get our old crowd together at my house this afternoon, have a regular reunion."

Liz's informal party grew like a snowball rolling down hill. The crowd took over the Kendall's rumpus room and yakked and played records and danced away the afternoon. If this was a sample of what the holidays were going to be, Marcy thought ecstatically, she couldn't complain. Steve was flatteringly attentive and she seemed to find him more attractive with each passing hour.

She was enjoying herself so much she wished the afternoon never had to end, but finally she felt constrained to glance at her watch. As she had feared, it was almost five.

"I hate to break this up," Marcy said regretfully, "but I've got to go home and start dinner. If you want to stay longer, Steve—"

"Of course I'll come with you," Steve broke in.

The sidewalk was covered with a thick white layer of snow when they reached the street. "It's like walking in cake frosting," Marcy smiled.

Arm in arm with Steve in the cold blue dusk, she felt happiness well up in her in a sweet tide. She wondered if Steve felt the same way. Their glances met and the little half-grin he gave her was all the answer she needed.

After a while Steve asked her, "About tonight, can you get away from your friend Mr. Tuttle by eight-thirty?"

"Of course," Marcy told him. "He's such an old dear he'd let me go whenever I wanted to. But I'd hate to disappoint him entirely. He counts on me Thursday nights."

"I count on you all the time," Steve gave her arm a little squeeze against his side. "Just remember that." He added, "I thought we might play some bridge with my parents tonight, unless there's something you'd rather do. They were complaining they haven't seen anything of you since I've been away."

"I'd like that," Marcy said. Somehow it made her feel good to know that Steve's parents had missed her.

They went on discussing plans for the days ahead, the parties to which they had been invited, the big New Year's Eve dance at the country club which would climax the holidays.

Marcy said, with a little rueful laugh, "So many wonderful things crowded into less than two weeks! I wish I could spread them out, make them last for months and months."

"Then I wouldn't be around to take you to all of them," Steve reminded. "Or wouldn't you care?"

"Of course I would," Marcy told him. "Having you home makes everything a lot more fun."

"That's how I hope you feel," Steve said. "It's the way I feel about you." He went on, "At school when I take other girls out, I find myself thinking about you, finding fault with my date mentally because she isn't you. As if it's her fault." He grinned crookedly.

"I'm glad," Marcy said softly.

Steve went on, doggedly pursuing his own train of thought, "And when I think about you back here, going out with other fellows—well, it makes me feel kind of sick inside."

Marcy's tone was gentle. "You really needn't worry."

"You went out with someone else last night," Steve insisted. "By the way, who was your date with? You never did get around to telling me."

"You never got around to asking," Marcy reminded. She went on then to explain about her friendship with Rick Whitney and how it had grown from a crazy sort of experiment Ken had talked her into trying.

"Oh, fine," Steve said. "If you can't think up enough ways to give me a bad time, your brother has to help you. And I figured he was my pal."

Marcy knew he was only kidding. Steve chuckled, remembering, "Seems to me it was due to some of Ken's screwy ideas on psychology that you and I discovered each other in a big way."

"I know," Marcy nodded. What a long time ago that had been. And how much had happened since to test Steve's and her liking for each other. Had Ken had any notion, she wondered, what he was starting? She pointed out, "This theory of his worked, too. Maybe his ideas aren't so crazy after all."

"Maybe not," Steve admitted. "But just let's keep your friendship with Rick on a high platonic plane, shall we? I don't mind your dating the guy, having a little fun while I'm away. But if I thought there was any danger of your preferring him to me—well, just don't, that's all."

"I won't," Marcy said meekly.

It was quite thrilling to have Steve order her around in such a positive way, especially when he was squeezing her arm close against his side and looking down at her as though he wanted very much to kiss her.

❦ NINETEEN ❦

Happy Holiday

STEVE DROPPED MARCY OFF AT THE HOS-
pital that night and said he'd be back for her at eight-
thirty. She found Mr. Tuttle, his parchmenty old face
creased in an expectant smile, waiting for her. He had
the chess board and carved wooden chessmen all ready
on his bedside table, along with another box of chocolates.

Marcy smiled as she helped herself to a butter cream,
"You know you're endangering my complexion as well as
my figure with all this candy, don't you?"

"Pretty girl like you," the old man assured her, "hasn't
a thing to worry about on either score. I'm only surprised you got here, with your young man home for
vacation and all."

"I couldn't miss our game," Marcy told him. "But I'll
leave a little early. Steve's picking me up."

"Then let's get goin'," Mr. Tuttle said, his bright dark
eyes glowing with pleased anticipation.

They played with enjoyment and concentration for the next hour. Marcy's game was improving under Mr. Tuttle's instruction, so that now she was able to offer him more stimulating competition. Once in a while, she even won.

But tonight wasn't one of those special occasions. Mr. Tuttle beat her soundly. "I don't think you had your whole mind on the game," he accused, with his dry little chuckle.

"I have got quite a lot to think about," Marcy admitted, laughing, too. "The holidays and all, Steve home, so much going on all the time."

"Tell me what all you got planned," Mr. Tuttle said.

And Marcy did so, since he really seemed interested. When she had finished, he observed, "Sounds like you got a mighty full schedule figured out. But then, that's what Christmas holidays are for, fun and jollity." There was a note of wistfulness, imperfectly concealed, in his voice.

Marcy told him, "I'll be up to see you for a little while Christmas afternoon. I'll bring my brother, too. He's figuring on stopping by sometime himself for a chess game with you."

The old face brightened. "I'd like that," Mr. Tuttle said. "Don't want to be a burden on you folks, though."

"You're not," Marcy assured him. "But I have to go now. Steve will be waiting for me."

She said good night and went out into the long empty corridor, shrugging into her coat. Her visit with Mr. Tuttle had left her with a warm little glow, as was always the case. He was such an indomitable old character, so much an individualist. She wondered how he was going to like the pair of bedroom slippers she had bought him for Christmas. Her mother had agreed that the gift was a good idea when Marcy mentioned it to her. "It'll aim his thoughts toward getting well and back on his feet again," Mom had said. "Sometimes an old person like that just sort of gives up and resigns himself to being bedfast. But we can't let that happen to Mr. Tuttle. He's got to walk again."

The nurse on night duty smiled at Marcy and said hello from her desk in the angle of the hall. "You certainly are good medicine for Mr. Tuttle," she told Marcy. "You have no idea how he looks forward to your visits. He was a little worried tonight for fear you wouldn't come."

"I couldn't let him down," Marcy said, "without any warning. He should know that."

The gray-haired nurse leaned confidentially forward, "Did he mention next Thursday to you?"

Marcy shook her head, mystified.

"It's his birthday," the head nurse told her. "He's planning to have a cake with candles and ice cream—the works!—and surprise you when you come. I just thought maybe I'd better warn you, so there wouldn't be any chance you'd fail him, it being such a busy time for a young girl like you."

"I'll be here," Marcy told her. "Thanks for telling me, though."

She was smiling as she walked on along the hall. As she passed the door of the waiting room on the first floor, someone rose and came toward her. Marcy's first impression was that it might be Steve, that he had decided to come inside instead of waiting out in front in the car as they had planned. But it wasn't Steve, it was Bruce Douglas, blond and easy-moving, who fell into step with her.

He said, smiling, "I figured you must be here, it being Thursday. But I didn't see your car out in the parking lot, so I thought maybe I could give you a lift home."

Bruce, Marcy had learned since their first encounter here, spent quite a bit of time with his father at the hospital. He planned to study medicine himself and found the atmosphere of the place vitally interesting. His presence now didn't surprise her.

But she explained about being picked up. They talked casually as he held the heavy door open for her and walked with her down the broad stone steps to the street. Steve got out of a car parked near the entrance and came toward them.

"Hi," Marcy greeted him, feeling her heart hurry a little just at the sight of his tall, broad-shouldered figure.

She introduced the two young men and they stood talking for a couple of minutes under the street light, buffeted by the wind. Then Bruce said good night and strode off toward the hospital parking lot, whistling cheerily.

As Steve slid into the car beside Marcy, he eyed her rather oddly. Then he asked, "Where did he come from? Was he visiting Mr. Tuttle, too?"

Marcy laughed. "No, his father's a doctor there. I'm always running into him. Once I gave him a lift and tonight he offered me one, when he didn't see our car around."

"Oh," Steve said. "Very considerate." But he didn't sound too happy about it.

Marcy tried to curb the little smile that pulled at her lips. During the Thanksgiving holidays, she'd been the one who was jealous and unreasonable. Was Steve suffering a touch of the same ailment now? Somehow the suspicion that he might be endeared him to her still more . . .

Christmas Eve Marcy went carolling with a crowd of friends. Standing in the soft drifted snow outside the various houses they stopped at, singing all the sweet old songs that seemed so much a part of Christmas, Marcy felt the deep, abiding sense of happiness the season always engendered in her. If only, she thought, people could always feel warm and close to each other as they did at this special time of year. If only some of its wonderful spirit could carry over into all the months to come, how fine it would be for the weary battered old world.

After their round of singing was over, the crowd went back to Marcy's and Ken's house for hot mulled cider and fruit cake and Christmas cookies in front of the roaring fire. The tree, which Marcy and Ken had decorated that afternoon, glittered with varicolored lights and silver tinsel. And under it all the intriguing packages had come out of hiding to be stacked in a gay drift of red and green and gold and silver.

The crowd didn't stay too late. They were having fun, but Christmas Eve wasn't a staying-out-late sort of time. Mom and Dad along with Marcy and Ken waved good night to them from the front door and the chill air echoed with cries of "Merry Christmas." Then all the Rhodeses wandered back to the living room, their arms affectionately across each other's shoulders.

Mom, who had arranged to trade time with one of the

unmarried nurses at the hospital and so wouldn't have to work on Christmas Day, said, "Isn't it wonderful to think we're all going to be together tomorrow?"

Dad nodded. "Like old times when the kids were little."

Ken agreed, yawning, "It'll be swell. But I'm for hitting the sack pretty soon. If I know my sister, she'll be up at the crack of dawn to see what she got for Christmas."

"Can I help it," Marcy laughed up at him, "if I'm just naturally curious?"

Christmas was absolutely perfect, Marcy felt, except in one respect. It was over too soon. From the moment when they all came trooping downstairs in robes and slippers, until bedtime that night, it seemed as though only an hour or so elapsed. So many things went to make up all the rush and confusion of a happy holiday. Gifts to open and admire. Dinner to get, working with Mom in the warm, delicious-smelling kitchen. Neighbors dropping in and lingering a little while, talking and laughing. Some calls for them to make on the Kendalls, the Judsons, and a few other old friends.

Marcy and Ken snatched half an hour from the busy day for a brief visit with Mr. Tuttle. His room looked quite festive, with the little silver tree the Hospital Guild had put on each patient's bedside table, and the flowers Mom and Dad had sent. Mr. Tuttle and Ken took to each other at once and made a date to play chess during visiting hours on Monday afternoon. Mr. Tuttle's old eyes lit at sight of Marcy's gift.

"Just see to it you wear these slippers soon," Marcy told him. "I don't want them wasted."

And the old man agreed, "I will. You'll see!" There was an indomitable set to his thin old shoulders, against the pillows of his bed.

He had a small package for Marcy, rather clumsily wrapped and with far too many Christmas stickers. The knowledge that he had fussed with it himself touched her. She could feel his anxious glance hurrying her fingers along as she opened it. There on a nest of white cotton lay a truly lovely little compact, with a filigree design of gold on silver, framing her initials.

"Why, Mr. Tuttle!" Marcy's eyes, lifting to his expectant face, were very bright. "It's beautiful!"

"You really like it?" he asked. "I had your Ma pick it out for me, figgered she'd know your tastes."

"It's absolutely perfect," Marcy told him. She leaned down to brush her lips against his wrinkled cheek. "I'll carry it at the New Year's Eve dance and every time I powder my nose, I'll think of you!"

Mr. Tuttle patted her hand. His eyes seemed brighter than usual, too . . .

When they were downstairs in the car once more, Ken said, "Not to get maudlin or anything, but that's a pretty nice thing you're doing for the old guy, going to see him every week."

Marcy smiled a little. "At first it was just something my conscience prodded me into—but I've grown to enjoy it myself. And you know, it's funny—" she broke off, thinking things through before she tried to put them into words, not wanting to sound, as Ken so aptly put it, maudlin.

After a minute she went on, "It's queer how things sort of hinge on each other. For instance, I started play-

ing chess with Mr. Tuttle and through that I got to know
Bruce Douglas. We haven't had a real date yet, but I
wouldn't be surprised if we do soon. We've got pretty
well acquainted, just through running into each other
at the hospital and talking more at school. And then
because you egged me on to make some effort, I got to
know Rick. And we've had several dates, ever so much
fun together."

"It sounds," Ken grinned at her, "as though things are
picking up for you, as if you've stopped just sitting
around brooding when Steve's away."

"I haven't got time to brood," Marcy told him, "even
though I am awfully fond of Steve. I think the thing is
—well, I've learned to be more adjustable. Instead of
letting everything throw me—Mom's working and Steve's
being away and all—I guess I've grown up enough to
make the best of things as they are."

"That's quite a bit of growing up," Ken commented
drily, "for a squirt your age. If I wasn't afraid of its
going to your head, I might even admit I'm as proud of
you as Mom and Dad are."

"Flattery will get you nowhere!" Marcy kidded. But a
warm little glow of satisfaction went through her at
Ken's words just the same.

As they drove home, Marcy told Ken a little more
about Rick and Bruce. And he talked quite a lot about
Lee Creighton. Poor Rosemary, Marcy thought. It
sounded as though Ken were simply passing the time
with her, until he got back to college and Lee. A horrible doubt suddenly assailed her.

She asked, "Do you think Steve still likes me best,

Ken?" It would be awful if she were in the same sorry position as Rosemary and didn't even know it.

"Why ask me?" Ken chuckled. "Hasn't he told you?"

Marcy said, "Maybe you're sweet-talking Rosemary, too. How do I know? And all the time you can't wait to get back to Lee. If Steve feels like that about me and Thea—"

Ken broke in firmly, "Don't be getting screwy notions. I told Rosemary about Lee. She knows how things stand. As for you and Steve," he chuckled, "if he preferred Thea, he could still see her during the holidays. She only lives over in Clay City. Didn't you know that?"

"No," Marcy said slowly. "Steve didn't tell me."

She'd had no idea how available Thea still was. Clay City—why, that was only half an hour's drive. Steve could have been seeing Thea right along, instead of spending all his time with her. The knowledge lit a bright flame of happiness in Marcy's heart.

But she hadn't realized how widely she was smiling, until Ken said, with a little chuckle, "If I'd known you'd be that pleased to hear it, I'd have told you long ago!"

❧ TWENTY ❧

Bitter Blow

ON SUNDAY, THE DAY AFTER CHRISTMAS, Rick Whitney phoned Marcy. Hearing his voice made her realize how seldom she had thought of him during the past few days. Steve had managed to put him almost completely out of her mind. When Rick asked her to go to the movies with him the following night, Marcy accepted the invitation without hesitancy.

"Swell," Rick said. "I wasn't sure you meant it when you said Steve Judson wouldn't monopolize all your time."

"Of course, I did," Marcy told him. But she felt a small nip of guilt as she said it. Would she have agreed so readily to go out with Rick, if she hadn't known that Steve and Ken were driving to Clay City Monday night for a stag party with some of their fraternity brothers?

As she hung up after her talk with Rick, the doorbell chimed and, when Marcy answered it, there was Liz. They gravitated up to Marcy's room, so that they wouldn't be interrupted, since both of them felt an urge for confidential conversation. Marcy's father and Ken were sprawled in the living room, giving the Sunday paper a second look. And Mom was working at the hospital, since she had to make up for taking Christmas Day off.

As soon as they were alone, Liz flopped down on the slipper chair and demanded, "What are you going to do about Rick while Steve's home?"

Marcy lay across the foot of her bed, her chin on her palms, her dark glance fixed thoughtfully on her friend's face. "I just got through making a date with him for tomorrow night," she answered, "although that doesn't really prove anything because—"

Liz gave her no chance to finish. "Good!" she broke in, beaming. "That's just the way I feel. I've got a date with Hank for tonight and Bill was furious when he heard about it."

"He was?" Marcy asked. "What did he say?"

"The air," Liz gestured graphically, "positively crackled. But I don't care. I said a few things, too. He's got a lot of nerve, imagining he can go away and not even write me for months and then come back and pick up right where we left off."

Marcy nodded in agreement. "Steve wrote to me quite often," she admitted. "But, even so, I don't see how he could expect me to simply ignore Rick all the time he's home and risk being left without anyone after he goes back to college. Even though I like Steve best—"

Once more Liz interrupted, her righteous indignation making her forget her manners. "I don't even like Bill best any more. Right at first that tan and those expansive Texas ways he's picked up sort of dazzled me. But actually Hank's got a lot nicer personality. Bill thinks he's an awfully big wheel since he went away to college, but that doesn't make me willing to go on being his hub cap!"

"You mean you're all through?" Marcy asked.

"Oh, no," Liz smiled faintly. "I wouldn't make it that final. Not till after the New Year's Eve dance. Bill's taking me to that. And when I talked back to the old big-shot, he kind of backed down a little. I let him know he didn't own me, that I still felt free to date Hank when I wanted to."

Marcy nodded. She mused thoughtfully, "I wonder if Steve would be sore if he knew I was going out with Rick. He didn't make an issue of it that night he got home."

"You never can tell how a man will react," Liz's tone was philosophical. "They aren't very consistent, if you ask me. But they certainly make life a lot more interesting."

With that final statement Marcy could wholeheartedly agree . . .

Late that afternoon, Steve dropped in without any advance warning. Marcy, who was sitting cross-legged on the floor, engaged in a hot game of "Dirty Eight" with Ken, scolded, "Why don't you ever call up and warn me you're coming? Then you wouldn't catch me looking like this."

"Nothing wrong with the way you look." Steve grinned, eyeing her plaid corduroy slacks and yellow sweater approvingly. "Is that a private game or can anybody play?"

"More the merrier," Ken gestured hospitably. "Pull up a piece of floor and sit down."

Marcy was reminded of their old casual afternoons of companionship when they had all been younger and Steve dropped in more often to see Ken than on her account. They played cards till the afternoon light faded. Dad got up from his nap and wandered downstairs to kibitz. Then Mom got home and invited Steve to stay for an informal Sunday night supper with them. He and Marcy did the dishes and afterward they all sat around in front of the fire, talking and listening to records.

When it was time for Steve to go, Marcy went to the door with him and they stood for a time in the hall, in a low-voiced conversation. The soft, slow music from the record player eddied about them, creating its gentle mood.

Steve asked, "You don't mind about tomorrow night, the stag thing?"

"Of course not," Marcy told him, swallowing a small qualm of guilt. But why should she go out of her way to tell him of her date with Rick? "I hope you have a grand time . . ."

She herself had a very pleasant evening in Rick's company. They saw a good show and drove around for a while afterward in Rick's old station wagon, stopping at a roadside grill for something to eat. She was used to Rick's quietness, it didn't make her feel uncomfortable at all. When he had something to say, he said it. Marcy felt sure he enjoyed the pleasant, undemanding friendship between them as much as she did.

The stag party, Marcy heard from Ken when he got up around eleven the next morning, had been a great success. Some half dozen of the brothers, who lived in or near Clay City, had dined together and had a bull session afterward that lasted far into the night, during which practically all the world's problems had been settled one way or another.

When Steve called up a little later, Marcy told him, "I hear you had quite a session last night."

"You're so right," Steve chuckled. And, after they had talked for a while about nothing in particular, he asked, "What did you do last night?"

Marcy knew there was no special point to his question. He was just making conversation. Still, she saw no reason not to answer honestly, "I saw a movie with Rick Whitney."

After a second of silence, Steve said, "Oh?" rather quizzically. He asked then, "Did you have fun?"

"Um-hum," Marcy said.

"More fun than when you go out with me?"

"No," Marcy told him. "But you were busy last night, remember?" It was such fun to tease Steve.

"That's right," he agreed. "But if I hadn't been busy, would you still have gone out with Rick?"

"Yes," Marcy said. "If he asked me first."

Steve's chuckle reached her ear along the wire. "When you're so honest, how can I get sore at you?"

Marcy was glad he felt that way about it. His attitude was much more mature than Bill Weaver's had been.

Steve asked then, "Did Ken tell you about the other big deal we cooked up last night?"

"No," Marcy said, interested, "what was that?"

Steve went on to explain. The boys had thought of a wonderful idea. They had made plans to bring their girls and meet for supper and an evening's entertainment and dancing at the Starlight Room, a night club at Clay City's biggest hotel.

"Sound like fun?" Steve asked.

"Oh, yes!" Marcy answered with mounting enthusiasm.

Steve supplied some more details and Marcy listened, enchanted. She had never been to the Starlight Room and it sounded terrific. Her eyes lit like candles and her breath came faster. A party at a night club, the New Year's Eve dance, all the fun and gayety she'd already had—how would she ever get down to earth and the ordinary routine of living after these wonderful holidays?

Finally Marcy thought to ask, "When is it to be, Steve?"

He laughed ruefully. "Didn't I tell you that? Absent-minded, that's me. It's Thursday night."

His words went echoing off down the corridors of Marcy's mind like the gong of doom. Thursday? But it couldn't be. Steve or Ken—one of them should have remembered that she couldn't do anything on Thursday nights, that she went to see Mr. Tuttle. And this particular Thursday, Marcy remembered, her throat aching with the stabbing knowledge, was the old man's birthday. A cake with candles, ice cream—the works, the night nurse had warned Marcy, all planned secretly as a surprise for her.

These thoughts raced pell-mell through Marcy's head, but the only word that rose to her lips was an appalled, rather high-pitched, "Thursday?"

Steve still didn't understand. "I know it's kind of an off night," he admitted, "but there's not much of the holidays left. And Friday's the New Year's Eve dance and New Year's Day wouldn't do and next Tuesday we have to leave for school, remember?"

Marcy remembered only too well. Still, all she could say, wetting her lips carefully for the effort was, "Steve, I can't go. Not on Thursday. I told you about Mr. Tuttle—"

"You're kidding!" Steve's tone was suddenly rather grim. "You mean you can't change nights this once? For something as special as this?"

Marcy said dully, "I can't change it." And she went to tell Steve why.

When she had finished, he said, "Gee, Marce, I'm sorry." His voice wasn't grim any more, just disappointed. "There isn't anything I can do to change the date now, though. It's all set."

"I know," Marcy murmured. "I understand how it is. I'm—sorry, too."

The understatement of the year, she thought wryly. She was sunk, hopelessly and completely.

"Yeah," Steve said and his tone told Marcy clearly he was feeling the same way she was. But he wasn't mad at her. Marcy felt proud of him for that. He was being very adult about it, not flying off the handle as some boys would have.

It occurred to her then that the least she could do was to let Steve know that she could act in an adult manner, too.

She said, her voice a little husky, but firm, "I don't see why you shouldn't go, Steve. You could ask another girl."

She didn't mention Thea's name. But Thea was so

very available, Thea lived right in Clay City. And Thea would no doubt leap at the chance to go to the Starlight Room with Steve and his friends. Thea would probably be more at home with them than she, Marcy, because Thea knew them all. Marcy blinked back the tears that pricked beneath her eyelids.

"You mean—you wouldn't care?" Steve asked.

"That would be pretty childish of me, wouldn't it?" A very neat way, Marcy thought, of evading an honest answer.

"Oh, I don't know," Steve said.

For a minute silence stretched along the telephone line. Then Marcy managed, "After all, it's not your fault I can't go. And you asked me first—so there's nothing for me to get mad about."

"I guess that's right," Steve said and it seemed to Marcy he didn't sound quite so glum as he had a minute before.

When she hung up a few moments later, Marcy headed instinctively for her own room. But tears overtook her long before she reached it. No matter, though, she realized, flinging herself face downward across her bed. Ken had gone out to the airport to see his friend Hank Carlson and talk about flying for a while. There was no one home but her.

At times, she thought, crying unashamedly, it was a very good thing to have the house all to herself.

❧ TWENTY-ONE ❧

Mr. Juttle's Birthday Party

BY THURSDAY, MARCY HAD MANAGED TO
build up a wall of equanimity against the hurt of knowing that Steve would be taking Thea to the Starlight
Room while she visited Mr. Tuttle. She had fashioned
the wall laboriously, section by section. The realization
that Steve had asked her first had gone into it, as had
the awareness that there was no reason for him to give
up the plan just because she couldn't go. Was this
ability to rationalize, to look at things sensibly, a part of
being grown up, Marcy wondered? She assumed that it
was, and so succeeded in choking down the childish little
hurt voice within her that cried out, It's not fair!

Ken dropped her off at the hospital on his way to pick
up Rosemary and Steve for the drive to Clay City. "How
will you get home?" he asked.

Marcy said, "If Bruce isn't around, I'll call a cab.
Don't worry. And have fun. Tell Steve I said to have
fun, too."

"Will do," Ken grinned. Marcy thought she detected admiration in the look he gave her, as well as sympathy. "I'm as sorry as Steve is that things worked out like this."

"I know," Marcy said, trying to sound very detached about it. "But it's just one of those things."

She waved as Ken drove off, then walked slowly up the broad stone steps of the hospital. By the time she reached Mr. Tuttle's room, she had her usual smile carefully arranged. A second later it widened into a look of genuine pleased astonishment.

Mr. Tuttle was not on his high white bed, his plaster cast dwarfing the rest of him into comparative insignificance. The old man sat, beaming delightedly at Marcy, in a wheel chair near the windows. And on his feet were the bedroom slippers she had given him for Christmas.

"Why, Mr. Tuttle!" Marcy gasped. "When did all this happen? Mom didn't tell me."

"I told her not to. Wanted to spring it on you myself." His smile growing even wider, Mr. Tuttle manipulated his chair back and forth, the while he supplied Marcy with a full account of the removal of his cast, and the wonderful way the bone had knit for a man of his age.

"And you know something else?" he demanded, motioning toward the screen that hid his bedside table. "Move that aside."

When Marcy did so, she was confronted by the not entirely surprising sight of a birthday cake of gargantuan proportions, complete with pink sugar roses and more candles than she could conveniently count.

She turned to stare at Mr. Tuttle with a nice imitation

of complete astonishment. "It's your birthday!" she exclaimed. "Why didn't you tell me?"

"Wanted to surprise you," he chuckled, as delighted as a child.

Marcy said a small prayer of thankfulness that she had let nothing interfere to spoil this shining moment for him.

"How many candles are there?" she asked.

"Not as many as there should be," he told her. "The cake wasn't big enough to hold seventy-four."

"Shall I light them now, for you to blow out?"

Mr. Tuttle nodded vigorously. "Then we can cut the cake. I told all the nurses I was havin' open house tonight, so some of 'em will be stoppin' in for refreshments."

Marcy lit the candles and sang "Happy Birthday." The lovely warm glow was no brighter than the glow in Mr. Tuttle's eyes as he huffed and puffed at them. Marcy helped him cut the cake and he rang for the nurse to bring in some ice cream. Nurses and internes kept dropping in all evening to eat cake and congratulate Mr. Tuttle.

The old man said, his speculative glance on Marcy, "Looks like your friend Bruce isn't around tonight. Haven't seen anything of him."

"I guess not," Marcy said.

"Right nice young feller," Mr. Tuttle pursued the subject. "I promised to teach him how to play chess. I think he's kind of sweet on you."

"Not really," Marcy smiled. "Bruce is friendly with everyone. He's very popular at school."

"He likes you, though," the old man argued good-naturedly. "I can tell. And that Steve you been seein' so much of lately—he must like you, too. Lots of girls as popular as you are with the boys wouldn't waste time on an old codger like me."

"Are you fishing for compliments?" Marcy asked, her tone mock-accusing. "It's your move and I think you're just killing time because you can see I've almost got you checkmated."

When visiting hours were over, Marcy said good night to Mr. Tuttle and went out into the hall. Despite the warm little glow within her, she couldn't shut out the thought of all she was missing. Nine o'clock—probably Steve was dancing with Thea right now.

And Bruce isn't even around to offer me a lift home, Marcy thought regretfully, as she fished a dime out of her wallet to call for a cab from the booth in the lobby downstairs.

As she passed the wide door of the waiting room, she heard the squeak of chair springs as someone rose hastily. Marcy's glance was only mildly questioning then her mouth dropped open just a little in complete astonishment. She stood there foolishly, her coin for the phone clutched in her fingers, staring up into Steve Judson's grinning face.

Without a word, he slipped his arm through hers and propelled her across the lobby and out into the windy night.

"Would you mind telling me," Marcy finally managed to ask, "what you're doing here?"

"Meeting you," Steve said. "Figuring on taking you for a little ride. Maybe even buying you a hamburger. Unless you have other plans?"

"Not a plan," Marcy admitted, as they walked toward the parking lot. Her heart was beating so fast she could scarcely speak. To have Steve here, with her, when she had been picturing him with Thea, when she had been so hurt and jealous way down inside, under all her mature pretense of unconcern. "Tell me what happened," she insisted.

"Nothing happened," Steve said, still grinning as he helped her into the car and slid in under the wheel beside her, "except that my girl was bent on doing her good deed, so what else could I do except pick her up afterward?"

"But what about Thea?" Marcy demanded. "And the Starlight Room and everything?"

Steve put his arm around her, gave her a quick hard hug that made Marcy's pulses race crazily. "Somehow I lost my taste for it when you couldn't go. At first I thought maybe I would ask Thea, but the more I thought about it, the less I wanted to. Ken figured I had asked her—he was sure surprised when I told him what I was going to do instead. He didn't really mind, though."

"I don't mind, either," Marcy told him. "But I meant it when I said you could take Thea. I wouldn't have been mad."

"Heck!" Steve said. "Wouldn't you have been real jealous?"

"Inside I would have been," Marcy admitted. "But I hope I'm too grown up to let it show."

"That's okay then," Steve said. "It's how you feel inside that interests me, anyway."

Marcy had never felt more drawn to Steve, never

thought him so wonderful as she did at that moment. But all she said was, "I think you're kind of crazy—but sweet."

Their glances met in a long look of understanding and his face came down toward hers. Just before their lips met, Steve murmured, "My opinion of you exactly."

🌿 THE END 🌿